D0031120

Also by Andrea Camilleri

To request Penguin Readers Guides by mail
(while supplies last), please call (800) 778-6425
or e-mail reading@us.penguingroup.com.
To access Penguin Readers Guides online,
visit our Web site at www.penguin.com.

Elvira Giorgianni

THE WINGS OF THE SPHINX

Andrea Camilleri is the author of many books, including his Montalbano series, which has been adapted for Italian television and translated into nine languages. He lives in Rome.

Stephen Sartarelli is an award-winning translator and the author of three books of poetry, most recently *The Open Vault*.

THE WINGS OF THE SPHINX

ANDREA CAMILLERI

Translated by Stephen Sartarelli

PENGUIN BOOKS

PENGUIN BOOKS

Published by the Penguin Group

Penguin Group (USA) Inc., 375 Hudson Street, New York, New York 10014, U.S.A.
Penguin Group (Canada), 90 Eglinton Avenue East, Suite 700, Toronto,
Ontario, Canada M4P 2Y3 (a division of Pearson Penguin Canada Inc.)
Penguin Books Ltd, 80 Strand, London WC2R 0RL, England
Penguin Ireland, 25 St Stephen's Green, Dublin 2, Ireland (a division of Penguin Books Ltd)
Penguin Group (Australia), 250 Camberwell Road, Camberwell,
Victoria 3124, Australia (a division of Pearson Australia Group Pty Ltd)
Penguin Books India Pvt Ltd, 11 Community Centre,
Panchsheel Park, New Delhi - 110 017, India
Penguin Group (NZ), 67 Apollo Drive, Rosedale, North Shore 0632,
New Zealand (a division of Pearson New Zealand Ltd)
Penguin Books (South Africa) (Pty) Ltd, 24 Sturdee Avenue,
Rosebank, Johannesburg 2196, South Africa

Penguin Books Ltd, Registered Offices:
80 Strand, London WC2R 0RL, England

First published in Penguin Books 2009

1   3   5   7   9   10   8   6   4   2

Translation copyright © Stephen Sartarelli, 2009
All rights reserved

Originally published in Italian as *Le ali della sfinge* by Sellerio Editore, Palermo.
Copyright © 2006 Sellerio Editore.

PUBLISHER'S NOTE

This is a work of fiction. Names, characters, places, and incidents either are the product
of the author's imagination or are used fictitiously, and any resemblance to actual persons,
living or dead, business establishments, events, or locales is entirely coincidental.

LIBRARY OF CONGRESS CATALOGING IN PUBLICATION DATA
Camilleri, Andrea.
[Ali della sfinge. English]
The wings of the Sphinx / Andrea Camilleri ; translated [from the Italian] by Stephen Sartarelli.
p. cm.—(A Penguin mystery)
ISBN 978-0-14-311660-8
1. Montalbano, Salvo (Fictitious character)—Fiction.   2. Police—Italy—Fiction.   3. Murder—
Investigation—Fiction.   4. Human trafficking victims—Fiction.   5. Catholic Church—
Charities—Fiction.   I. Sartarelli, Stephen, 1954–   II. Title.
PQ4863.A3894A6513 2010
853'.914—dc22   2009029581

Printed in the United States of America
Set in Bembo   Designed by Jaye Zimet

THE WINGS OF THE SPHINX

1

What ever happened to those early mornings when, upon awakening, for no reason, he would feel a sort of current of pure happiness running through him?

It wasn't the fact that the day was starting out cloudless and windless and the sun shining bright. No, it was a different sensation, one that had nothing to do with his meteoropathic nature. If he had to explain, it was like feeling in harmony with all of creation, perfectly synchronized with a great stellar clock precisely positioned in space, at the very point that had been destined for him since birth.

Bullshit? Fantasy? Maybe.

But the indisputable fact was that he used to have this feeling rather often, whereas now, for the last few years, it was so long, nice knowing you. Gone. Vanished. In fact, nowadays early mornings very often inspired a feeling of refusal in him, a sort of instinctive rejection of what awaited him once he was forced to accept the new day, even if there were no particular hassles awaiting him in the hours ahead. And the proof of this was the way he acted upon emerging from sleep.

Now the moment he raised his eyelids, he immediately lowered them again, remaining in darkness for a few more seconds, whereas before, the moment he opened his eyes, he kept them open, even slightly agape, avidly taking in the light of day.

And this, he thought, *is surely because of my age.*

But immediately Montalbano Two rebelled against this conclusion.

Because, for a few years now, two different Montalbanos lived inside the inspector, and they were always in disagreement. The moment one of them said something, the other would assert the opposite. And indeed, as if on cue:

What's this about your age? said Montalbano Two. *How is it possible that, at fifty-six, you already feel old? You want to know the real truth?*

No, said Montalbano One.

Well, I'm going to tell you anyway. You want to feel old because it suits you just fine. Since you've grown tired of what you are and what you do, you've created this excuse about getting old. But if you really feel that way, why don't you write a nice letter of resignation right now and call it quits?

And what would I do then?

You would play the old man. Get yourself a dog to keep you company, go out in the morning to buy the newspaper, sit down on a bench, let the dog run free, and start reading the paper, beginning with the death notices.

Why the death notices?

Because whenever you read that someone your age has just died while you're still fairly alive, you'll feel a certain satisfaction that'll help you hang around for at least another twenty-four hours. An hour later—

An hour later you and your dogs can go fuck yourselves, said Montalbano One, chilled by the prospect.

Well, then, get up, go to work, and stop being a pain in the ass, Montalbano Two concluded decisively.

While he was in the shower the telephone rang. He went to answer it completely naked, leaving a stream of water in his wake. Adelina, in any case, would be by later to clean house.

"Chief, whadd I do, wake y'up?"

"No, Cat, I was awake."

"You sure sure sure 'bout that, Chief? Yer not jess sayin' 'at to be nice?"

"No, you needn't worry. What is it?"

"Chief, what else could it be if I'm callin' you foist ting in the morning?"

"Cat, do you realize that you never call to give me any good news?"

There was a pause, and then Catarella's voice became all choked up.

"Ah Chief Chief! Whyddya say that? You wanna humiliate me? If it was up to me, I'd wake you up every single mornin' wit' rilly good news, like, I dunno, like you jess won tirty billions inna lattery, or like you was jess made chief o' police, or . . ."

Not having heard the door open, the inspector suddenly saw Adelina standing before him, staring at him, keys still in hand. Why had she come so early? Embarrassed, he instinctively turned towards the telephone to hide his privates. Apparently the male backside is considered less shameful than the front. The housekeeper quickly fled into the kitchen.

"Cat, wanna bet I know why you're calling? A dead man was found somewhere. Am I right?"

"Yes and no, Chief."

"Where am I wrong?"

"Iss a dead lady, Chief."

"Listen, isn't Inspector Augello around?"

"He's a'ready atta scene o' the crime, Chief. But the inspector jess called me now sayin' to call you now, Chief, sayin' as how iss bitter if you go there, too, Chief, poissonally in poisson."

"Where was she found?"

"Atta Sarsetto, Chief, round about the 'Murcan bridge."

That was far along the road to Montelusa. And the inspector had no desire to get behind the wheel.

"Send a car over to pick me up."

"The cars're all inna garage and can't go nowheres, Chief."

"They all broke down at the same time?"

"Nossir, Chief, they's workin' all right. But the fack is there's no more money to buy gasoline. Fazio called Montelusa but they tol' 'im to be patient 'cause the money's onna way an'll be here in a few days, but not much ... So fer now only the flyin' squad can drive, an' Deputy Garruso's escort."

"His name is Garrufo, Cat."

" 'Is name is what 'is name is. All 'at matters is you unnastand who I mean, Chief."

The inspector cursed the saints. The police stations had no gasoline, the courts had no paper, the hospitals had no thermometers, and meanwhile the government was thinking about building a bridge over the Strait of Messina. But there was always plenty of gasoline for the useless escorts of ministers, vice ministers, undersecretaries, committee chairmen, senators, chamber deputies, regional deputies, cabinet chiefs, and underassistant briefcase carriers ...

"Have you informed the prosecutor, Forensics, and Dr. Pasquano?"

"Yessir. But Dr. Quaspano got rilly rilly pissed off."

"Why?"

"He says how since he ain't bibiquitous, he can't get to the scene for a couple a hours. Chief, could you asplain sumpin a me?"

"Sure, Cat."

"Whass bibiquitous mean?"

"It means being in many different and faraway places at the same time. Tell Augello I'm on my way."

He went into the bathroom and got dressed.

"Coffee's ready," Adelina informed him.

As soon as he walked into the kitchen, the housekeeper looked him up and down and said:

"You know you're still a good-lookin' man, signore?"

Still? What was that *still* supposed to mean? Montalbano darkened. But then Montalbano Two immediately appeared.

Oh, no, you don't! You can't get pissed off! You're contradicting yourself, considering that barely an hour ago you felt old and decrepit!

Better change the subject.

"Why'd you come early today?"

" 'Cause I gotta catch a bus to Montelusa to go talk to Judge Sommatino."

He was the judge overseeing the prison where Pasquale, the younger of the housekeeper's two sons, was being "detained." Pasqualino was a habitual offender whom Montalbano himself had arrested twice, and for whose firstborn son the inspector had been made godfather at the baptism.

" 'Parently the judge is gonna put inna good word so's he can come a home for house arrest."

The coffee was good.

"Lemme have another cup, Adelì."

Since Dr. Pasquano was going to be arriving late, he might as well take his time.

In the days of the Greeks, the Salsetto had been a river. Later, in the days of the Romans, it became a brook, then a rivulet by the time of Italian unification, and later still, in the Fascist era, a stinking little trickle, before finally becoming, with the advent of democracy, an illegal dumping ground. During the Allied invasion in 1943, the Americans built a metal bridge over the now-dried-up riverbed, but one night a few years later the span disappeared, having been entirely dismantled between sunrise and sunset by iron thieves. The spot, however, had retained the name.

The inspector pulled up in a clearing where there were already five police cars, two private vehicles, and the van for transporting corpses to the morgue. The squad cars all belonged to Montelusa Central Police; of the private cars, one belonged to Mimì Augello, the other to Fazio.

"How come in Montelusa they've got gasoline up the ass and we don't have a drop?" the inspector asked himself aloud, feeling annoyed.

He chose not to answer.

Augello came up as soon as he saw him get out of the car.

"Mimì, couldn't you have scratched your balls by yourself?"

"Salvo, I'm not going to play your game anymore."

"What do you mean?"

"I mean that, if I hadn't had you come here, later you'd be driving me crazy saying, Why didn't you tell me this, why didn't you tell me that . . . ?"

"What's the corpse like?"

"Dead," said Augello.

"Mimì, a quip like that is worse than a shot in the back. Fire off another, and I'll shoot you in self-defense. I'll ask you again: What's the corpse like?"

"Young. Barely more than twenty. Possibly foreign. And she must have been beautiful."

"Have you identified her?"

"Are you kidding? She's completely naked and there aren't any clothes about, not even a handbag."

They walked to the edge of the clearing.

A sort of narrow goat path led down to the dump some thirty feet below. Right at the bottom of the path stood a group of people, among whom the inspector recognized Fazio, the chief of Forensics, and Dr. Pasquano, who was bent over what looked like a mannequin. Prosecutor Tommaseo, on the other hand, was standing in the middle of the path and spotted the inspector.

"Wait, Montalbano, I'll be right there."

"What's going on? Is Pasquano here?" said Montalbano.

Mimì gave him a confused look.

"Why wouldn't he be here? He got here half an hour ago."

Apparently the doctor's blow-up at poor Catarella had all been for show.

Pasquano was famous for having a nasty disposition, and he was very keen on being known as an impossible man. Sometimes he took great pleasure in hamming it up just to maintain his reputation.

"Aren't you coming down?" asked Tommaseo, panting as he climbed up.

"What for? You've already seen her yourself."

"She must have been very beautiful. Fantastic body," said the prosecutor, eyes glistening with excitement.

"How was she killed?"

"A bullet to the face from a high-caliber revolver. She's absolutely unrecognizable."

"Why do you think it was a revolver?"

"Because the guys from Forensics can't find the shell."

"What happened, in your opinion?"

"Why, it's obvious, my friend! Plain as day! Clearly, the couple pulls up in the clearing, gets out of the car, takes the path down to the dry riverbed, which is more secluded. The girl takes her clothes off and then, after sexual inter-course . . ."—he stopped, licked his lips, and swallowed at the thought of intercourse—"the man shoots her right in the face."

"And why would he do that?"

"I dunno. That's what we're going to find out."

"Listen, was there a moon?"

Tommaseo gave him confused look.

"Well, it wasn't a romantic encounter, you know, there wasn't any need for moonlight, they were just there to—"

"I think I know what they were there to do, sir. What I meant was that, since these past few nights there hasn't been any moonlight, we should have found two corpses, not one."

Tommaseo now looked utterly lost.

"Why two?"

"Because climbing down that path in total darkness, they would certainly have broken their necks."

"But, what are you saying, Montalbano? Surely they had a flashlight! Of course they'd planned the whole thing out! Well, unfortunately I have to go now. I'll be hearing from you. Good day."

"Do *you* think that's the way it went?" Montalbano asked Mimì after Tommaseo had gone.

"If you ask me, it's just another of Tommaseo's sexual fan-tasies! Why would they go down into a dump to have sex? It stinks so bad down there you can't even breathe! And there are rats big enough to eat the flesh off your bones! They could have easily done it right here, in this clearing, which is famous for all the fucking that goes on every night! Have you had a look around at the ground? It's a sea of condoms!"

"Did you point this out to Tommaseo?"

"Of course. But you know what he answered?"

"I can imagine."

"He said that it's possible those two went to fuck in the dump because it was more thrilling to do it surrounded by shit. A taste for depravity, get it? The kind of thing that only enters the mind of someone like Tommaseo!"

"Okay. But if the girl wasn't a professional whore, it's possible that, with all the cars in this clearing and all the trucks passing by, she—"

"The trucks that go to the dump don't come through here, Salvo. They discharge their stuff on the other side, where there's an easier descent that somebody made specifically for heavy vehicles."

Fazio's head popped up at the top of the path.

"Good morning, Chief."

"Are they going to be here much longer?"

"No, Chief, another half an hour or so."

The inspector didn't feel like seeing Vanni Arquà, chief of Forensics. He felt a visceral antipathy towards him, and the feeling was entirely mutual.

"Here they come," said Mimì.

"Who?"

"Look over there," replied Augello, pointing towards Montelusa.

Over the dirt path connecting the provincial road to the dump there rose a big cloud that looked just like a tornado.

"*Matre santa*, the press!" exclaimed the inspector.

Obviously somebody from the commissioner's office had spilled the beans.

"I'll see you guys at the office," he said, racing towards his car.

"I'm going back down," said Augello.

The real reason he hadn't gone down into the dump was that he didn't want to see what he would have had to see. Augello had said the corpse was of a girl barely more than twenty years old. It used to be that he felt afraid of dying people, while the dead made no impression on him. Now, however, and for the past few years, he could no longer bear the sight of people cut down in their youth. Something inside him utterly rebelled against what he considered an act against nature, a sort of ultimate sacrilege, even if the young victim had been a crook or a murderer in turn. To say nothing of children! The moment the evening news displayed the mangled bodies of little children, killed by war, famine, or disease, he would turn off the television at once ...

"It's your frustrated paternal instinct," was Livia's conclusion, stated with a good dose of malice, after he had confided this problem to her.

"I have never heard of frustrated paternal instincts, only frustrated maternal instincts," he had retorted.

"Well, if it's not frustrated paternal instincts," Livia insisted, "maybe it means you have a grandfather complex."

"How can I have a grandfather complex if I've never been a father?"

"What's that got to do with it? Ever heard of an hysterical pregnancy?"

"It's when a woman has all the signs of being pregnant but isn't."

"Right. And you're having an hysterical grandfatherhood."

Naturally the argument had ended in a nasty squabble.

From the front doorway of the police station the inspector heard Catarella speaking frantically.

"No, Mr. C'mishner, sir, the inspector can't come to the phone 'cause he in't bibiquitous. He's at the Sarsetto in so much as— Hullo? Hullo? Whaddhe do, hang up? Hallo?"

He saw Montalbano.

"Ahhh Chief Chief! 'At was the c'mishner!"

"What'd he want?"

"He din't say, Chief. He said only as how he wanted a talk to you rilly emergently."

"Okay. I'll call him later."

On his desk was a mountain of papers to be signed. His heart sank at the sight. It really wasn't his day. He turned heel and passed by Catarella's closet.

"I'll be right back. I'm going to have a coffee."

After the coffee, he smoked a cigarette and went for a short walk. Then he returned to his office and called the commissioner.

"Montalbano here. Your orders, sir."

"Don't make me laugh!"

"Why, what did I do?"

"You said: 'Your orders, sir'!"

"So? What was I supposed to say?"

"It's not what you say that matters, it's what you do. I give the orders, you can be sure of that, but I can't—I don't dare—imagine what you do with them!"

"Mr. Commissioner, sir, I would never allow myself to do what you think I do with them."

"Let's drop it, Montalbano, it's better that way. What ever happened with that Piccolo business?"

Montalbano was befuddled. What piccolo business? He didn't know of any piccolo makers in Vigàta.

"Uh, Mr. Commissioner, I don't know of any musical-instrument makers in—"

"For God's sake, Montalbano! What are you talking about? Giulio Piccolo is a person, not an instrument; he's retired, seventy years old, and . . . Listen, Montalbano, listen very carefully to what I'm about to say, and you can take this as an ultimatum: I demand a thorough, written report on the matter by tomorrow morning."

He hung up. Surely the file on this Giulio Piccolo, about whom he couldn't remember a single thing, must be buried somewhere in that mountain of paper in front of him. Did he have the courage to set his hand to it? Ever so slowly, he extended his right arm and, with a lightning-quick jab—as you might make to grab a poisonous animal that could bite you—he grabbed the folder at the top of the pile. He opened it and his jaw dropped. It was none other than the file on Giulio Piccolo. He felt like falling to his knees and thanking Saint Anthony, who must certainly have worked this miracle. He opened the folder and started reading. Mr. Piccolo's fabric shop had burned down. The firemen had determined the cause to be arson. Mr. Piccolo declared that the shop was set on fire because he had refused to pay protection money. The police, on the other hand, believed that it was Piccolo himself who had set fire to his shop to collect the insurance. There was, however, something that didn't make sense. Giulio Piccolo was born in Licata, lived in Licata, and his shop was located on the main street of Licata. So why was this case not being handled by the Licata police instead of Vigàta's? The answer was simple: Because at Montelusa Central, they had confused Licata with Vigàta.

The inspector picked up a ballpoint, a sheet of paper with Vigàta Police letterhead, and wrote:

Respected Mr. Commissioner,
As Vigàta is not Licata, nor Licata Vigàta, there's been an error
of position, sir. What seems to you inaction, on the order you gave,
is nothing at all save respect for jurisdiction.

He signed it and stamped it. Bureaucracy had reawakened a long-lost poetical vein in him. True, the lines stumbled a bit, but Bonetti-Alderighi would never notice that he had answered him in rhyme. The inspector called Catarella, gave him the Piccolo file and the letter, telling him to send the lot to the commissioner after properly registering it according to protocol.

2

Shortly after Catarella went out, Mimì Augello, back from the dump, appeared in the doorway. His nerves looked frayed.

"Come on in. Did you finish up?"

"Yes." He sat down on the edge of the chair.

"What's wrong, Mimì?"

"I have to run home. On my way here Beba rang to tell me she needs me because Salvuzzo's crying with a tummy ache and she can't seem to calm him down."

"Does he often have this problem?"

"Often enough to bust my balls."

"Your attitude doesn't seem very fatherly to me."

"If you had a son as annoying as mine, you'd have him flying out the window."

"But wouldn't Beba do better to call a doctor instead of you?"

"Of course. But Beba can't take a step without having me beside her. She's incapable of making any sort of decision on her own."

"Okay, tell me what you have to tell me, and you can go home."

"I managed to talk a little with Pasquano."

"Did he tell you anything?"

"You know what he's like. He takes every little killing

personally. Like some sort of offense, some slight to himself. And it gets worse with each passing year. Jesus, what a nasty disposition!"

Deep down, Montalbano felt he understood Pasquano perfectly.

"Maybe he can't stand cutting up corpses anymore. So, tell me."

"Between the curses, I was able to make him tell me that, in his opinion, the girl wasn't killed where her body was found."

"Wait a second. Who was it that found her?"

"Somebody named Salvatore Aricò."

"And what was he doing around there at the crack of dawn?"

"The guy goes to the dump every day, first thing in the morning, to look for things that can be salvaged, which he then fixes up and resells. He told me that nowadays the stuff he finds is practically brand-new, hardly used at all."

"You just now discovering consumerism, Mimì?"

"As soon as he got there, Aricò saw the body and called us on his cell phone. When I questioned him, I realized he didn't know any more than he'd already told us, so I had him give me his address and telephone number and let him go, because, among other things, the guy was really upset and kept throwing up."

"You were saying that, according to Pasquano, the girl was killed at another location."

"Right. There was practically no trace of blood anywhere around the body. Whereas there should have been, and a lot. In addition, Pasquano noticed that the body was scuffed and bruised in a number of spots, likely because when it was thrown from the clearing, it got banged around as it rolled down the slope.

"Couldn't these scuffs have been sustained during a struggle prior to the killing?"

"For the moment Pasquano rules that out."

"And he's seldom wrong. Was any blood found in the clearing where the cars pull up?"

"No, not there, either."

"That would confirm Pasquano's thesis that she was brought there after she was killed. Maybe in the trunk of a car. Could the doctor tell how long she's been dead?"

"That was the best part. He says he won't know with any certainty until after the autopsy, but at a glance, he would say she was killed at least twenty-four hours before she was found."

Which was strange enough in itself.

"But why would anyone keep a corpse hidden for an entire day?"

Mimì threw up his hands.

"I really couldn't tell you, but that's what it looks like. And there's another thing that might—I say, might—be important. The body was lying on its back, but at a certain point Pasquano flipped it over."

"So?"

"On the left shoulder, near the shoulder blade, she had a tattoo of a butterfly."

"Well, that might help identify the body. Did Forensics get some shots of it?"

"Yes. And I told them to send us the photos. But it's not like I have a lot of hope."

"Why?"

"Salvo, do you remember how, before I got married, I used to have a different girlfriend every couple of days?"

"Yes, you would have made Don Juan die of envy. And so?"

"The most popular tattoo among girls these days is butterflies. They have them tattooed in every imaginable part of their bodies. Just think, one time I actually discovered a butterfly tattooed right in the—"

"Spare me the details," the inspector implored him. "Say hi to Beba for me and send me Catarella."

Who showed up ten minutes later.

" 'Scuse me, Chief, but Cuzzaniti wasted a lotta time wit' the prototol. He coun't figger out if the nummer he was asposta give the file was treetousandsevenhunnert and five or treetousandsevenhunnert and six. Then me 'n' Cuzzaniti found the solution."

"What number did you give it?"

"We gave it both nummers, Chief. Treetousandsevenhunnert and fifty-six."

There was no way that file would ever be found again, were they to look for it for a hundred years.

"Listen, Cat. Check the list of missing persons on the computer and see if there's a report on a girl of about twenty with a butterfly tattooed near her left shoulder blade."

"What kind of butterfly, Chief?"

"How the hell should I know, Cat? A butterfly."

"I'm gonna go 'n' come back, Chief."

Fazio arrived. He came in and sat down.

"What have you got to tell me?" asked Montalbano.

"Dr. Pasquano is convinced that the girl—"

"—was killed somewhere else, I know. Augello already told me. And what do *you* think?"

"I agree. I've even come to the precise conclusion that the girl was stripped naked *after* she was murdered."

"What makes you think that?"

"Because if she'd been killed when she was naked, her

17

neck and shoulders and tits would have been covered in blood. Instead they were clean. And bear in mind that it hasn't rained for a week."

"I see. So the blood ended up on the clothes she was wearing at that moment, but not on her skin."

"Right. The body also had some abrasions, contusions, and lacerations from having been thrown down naked into the dump. If she'd been clothed, she would have suffered less damage. On top of that, she'd been bitten."

Montalbano gave a start. He immediately felt a wave of nausea in the pit of his stomach.

"What do you mean, she was bitten? Where?"

"She had three bites inside her right thigh. But Dr. Pasquano didn't want to talk to me about it; he doesn't know if they were human or animal bites."

"Let's hope it was an animal."

This was all they needed. A murderer who was also a werewolf. Half man, half animal.

"Did he say when he was going to do the autopsy?"

"Early tomorrow morning."

Catarella came in breathless, a sheet of paper in hand.

"I only foun' one girl around twenny, an' I prinnet up 'er pitcher. But there's nuttin' 'bout no buttafly inna report."

"Give it to Fazio."

Fazio took the sheet, glanced at it, and gave it back to Catarella.

"That's not her."

"How can you be so sure?" the inspector asked.

"'Cause this girl's brunette and the dead girl was blond."

"Couldn't she have dyed her hair?"

"Gimme a break, Chief."

Catarella slinked out, disappointed.

"I don't know why, but I don't think this girl was a whore," said Fazio.

"Maybe because nowadays it's very hard to say who's a whore."

Fazio gave him a befuddled look.

"Chief, a whore's always been a woman who sells her body, not just nowadays."

"That's too easy, Fazio."

"What do you mean?"

"Lemme give you an example. Take a twenty-year-old girl, a beautiful girl from a poor family. Somebody offers to put her in the movies, but she refuses, 'cause she's a respectable girl, and she's afraid she might get corrupted by that world. Then she meets some fifty-year-old businessman, pretty ugly but extremely rich, who wants to marry her. The girl accepts. She doesn't love the man, she doesn't find him attractive, and there's too much difference in age between them, but she thinks that over time she could grow fond of him. They get married and, as a wife, her conduct is irreproachable. Now, according to your definition, when the girl decided to say yes to the businessman, wasn't she selling her body for money? Of course she was. But are you ready to call her a whore?"

"Jesus Christ, Chief! I merely ventured an opinion, and you've written a whole novel about it!"

"All right, forget about it. What makes you think she didn't practice the profession?"

"Dunno. She wasn't wearing any lipstick. Or makeup. She was well groomed and clean, of course, but not excessively . . . Bah. What can I say? It was just my impression. But do me a favor and don't make another novel out of my impression."

"Listen, when's Forensics going to send us the photographs?"

"This afternoon."

"So I can go. I'll see you later."

When he got to the trattoria, he found the rolling metal shutter half lowered. He bent down and entered. The tables were all set but completely empty. There were no smells coming from the kitchen. Enzo, the owner and waiter, was sitting and watching television.

"How come there's nobody here?"

"Inspector, first of all, today's Monday, our day off, though you forgot. And secondly, it'd be a little early anyway, since it's not even twelve-thirty."

"Then I guess I'll go."

"Not a chance! Sit down!"

If it wasn't even twelve-thirty, why was he so ravenously hungry? Then he remembered he hadn't eaten the night before.

Because of a long and belligerent phone call from Livia, who had got it in her head to draw up a bankrupt balance sheet of their life together, interspersed with mutual accusations and apologies, he had completely forgotten about the skillet that Adelina had set on the stove for him to reheat what she had prepared for him. Afterwards, in his agitation over the phone call he no longer even felt like sating himself with the tumazzo cheese and olives he would certainly have found in the refrigerator.

"I got some langoustes, Inspector, that are a sight to behold."

"Big or small?"

"However you like."

"Bring me a big one. But only boiled, with nothing on it. And for a first course, if it's not too much trouble, bring me a generous portion of spaghetti with clam sauce, white, that is."

That way, with no strong flavor of sauces in his mouth, he could better savor the langouste, dressed only with olive oil and lemon.

As he was about to set to the langouste, images of the illegal dump appeared on the television screen. The cameraman framed the body, covered by a white sheet, from the clearing above.

"A horrific crime . . . ," began a voice off-camera.

"Turn that off at once!" the inspector yelled.

Enzo turned off the television and looked at him in astonishment.

"What's wrong, Inspector?"

"I'm sorry," said Montalbano. "It's just that . . ."

How quickly people had become cannibals!

Ever since television had entered the home, everyone had grown accustomed to eating bread and corpses. From noon to one o'clock, and from seven to eight-thirty in the evening— that is, when people were at table—there wasn't a single television station that wasn't broadcasting images of bodies torn apart, mangled, burnt, or tortured, men, women, old folks, and little children, imaginatively and ingeniously slaughtered in one part of the world or another.

Not a day went by without there being, in one part of the world or another, a war to broadcast to one and all. And so one saw people dying of hunger, who haven't got a cent to buy a loaf of bread, shooting at other people likewise dying of hunger, with bazookas, Kalashnikovs, missiles, bombs, all ultramodern weapons costing far more than medicine and food for everyone would have cost.

He imagined a dialogue between a husband sitting down to eat and his wife.

What'd you make today, Catarina?

For the first course, pasta with a sauce of children disemboweled by bombs.

Good. And for the main course?

Veal with a dressing of marketplace blown up by a suicide bomber.

Gee, Cata, I'm already licking my fingers!

Trying to preserve the taste of the langouste as long as possible between his tongue and palate, he set out on his customary stroll to the end of the jetty.

At the halfway point there was, without fail, the usual fisherman with his line. They greeted one another, and the angler warned him:

"Inspector, you oughta know that tomorrow is gonna be cold with heavy rain. An' iss gonna stay that way for a whole week."

The man had never been wrong in his predictions.

Montalbano's dark mood, which the langouste had managed to bring up to a tolerable level, became worse than before.

Was it possible the weather itself had gone crazy? How could it be that one week you were dying from heat at the equator and the following week you were freezing to death at the North Pole? *O siccu o saccu?* Was it all or nothing? Was there no longer a reasonable middle path?

He sat down on his favorite rock, the flat one, fired up a cigarette. And he started thinking.

Why had the killer gone and thrown the girl's body into the dump?

Certainly not to prevent it from being found or to hide it.

The killer knew perfectly well that the corpse was sure to be discovered a few hours later. On the other hand, he had done everything he could to delay the girl's identification as long as possible. Thus he had brought her to the dump merely to get rid of her.

But if he'd been able to keep her in the place where he'd killed her for a whole day without anyone discovering the body, why hadn't he left her there?

Maybe it wasn't a safe place.

How wasn't it safe?

And if the murderer had been able to kill the girl and hold on to the body for a long time without anyone noticing, why would he do something so dangerous as to take it to the dump? There could only be one reason: necessity. He had to move the body. But why?

The answer came to him from the langouste. Or, more precisely, from an aftertaste of langouste that resurfaced from the far reaches of his tongue. Enzo's trattoria had been closed when he got there because it was Monday. And since it was Monday, this meant that the girl had been killed Saturday, kept in the same place for all of Sunday, and then taken to the dump during the night between Sunday and Monday. Or, more likely, very early Monday morning, when there were no more cars of whores or johns in the clearing above the dump.

What did it mean?

It meant, he told himself proudly, that the place where the girl was killed must be a location that was closed on Saturday afternoons and all of Sunday, but reopened to the public on Monday morning.

His sudden enthusiasm over the conclusion he'd arrived at quickly waned when he realized just how many establishments were closed Saturday afternoons and Sundays: schools, government offices, private offices, doctors' offices, factories, notaries' offices, workshops, wholesale and retail stores, dentists' offices, warehouses, stores, tobacco shops ... Which amounted to slightly less than all of Vigàta. Actually, if he really thought about it, it was even worse than that. Because the murder could have been committed in any private home whatsoever, by a husband who had sent his wife and children off to the country for the weekend. In short, an hour of reflection for nothing.

When he returned to the station, he found an envelope from Forensics with the photos, two copies of each. The inspector didn't like Arquà; the very sight of him sent his cojones into a spin, but he honestly had to admit that the man did his job well.

Together with the photos was a memo. With no "dear" or greeting of any sort. But he himself would have done the same.

Montalbano,

The girl was definitely killed by a high-caliber firearm. Whether it was a revolver or a pistol is, for the moment, utterly irrelevant. The shot was fired from relatively close range, fifteen to twenty feet, and thus had devastating results. The bullet entered through the left jawbone and exited just below the right temple, following an upward trajectory, rendering the victim's facial features completely unrecognizable. I think the conclusions Dr. Pasquano draws from this will be very useful to you.

Arquà

When alive, the girl must have been a real beauty. One didn't have to be a connoisseur like Mimì Augello to realize this.

At a glance, she looked to be about five-foot-eleven. Blond. In her fall, her long hair, which must certainly have been gathered on her head in some kind of bun when she was killed, had come partly undone and covered the face that was no longer there. She had endless legs, like a dancer or athlete.

Montalbano took another look at the full-figure shots, then paused to dwell on those highlighting the tattoo. It was a decent enlargement of the image of the butterfly.

He put one of these in his jacket pocket, along with another one of the girl's back in which the tattooed shoulder blade was clearly visible.

"I'll be back in a couple of hours," he said to Catarella as he passed in front of him before going out.

He parked his car in front of the Free Channel's television studios, but before going in, he fired up a cigarette. Smoking was not allowed inside. And he always conformed—perhaps with a curse—whenever he saw a "No Smoking" sign.

On the other hand, where on earth was a poor bastard allowed to smoke these days? Not even in the toilets. The person who came in after you would smell the smoke and give you a dirty look. Because, in the twinkling of an eye, whole legions of fanatical smoke-haters had formed. Once, when he happened to be passing through a park with a cigarette in his mouth, he had intervened to separate two distinguished-looking eighty-year-old men who, for no apparent reason, had taken to clubbing each other on the head. Unable to break up the fight, so enraged were they, he had identified himself as a police inspector. And so the two elderly gentlemen immediately allied themselves against him.

"You ought to be ashamed of yourself!"

"You're smoking!"

"And you call yourself an officer of the law!"

"When in fact you're a smoker."

He had walked away, letting the two geezers resume breaking each other's head with their canes.

3

"Good morning, Inspector," said the girl at the entrance the moment she saw him walk in.

"Good morning. Is my friend in?"

At the Free Channel, Montalbano was one of the family.

"Yes, he's in his office."

He walked the length of the corridor, reached the last door, and knocked.

"Come in!"

He went in. Nicolò Zito looked up from a sheet of paper he was reading, recognized Montalbano, and stood up smiling.

"Salvo! What a nice surprise!"

They embraced.

"How are Taninè and Francesco?" asked the inspector, sitting down on a chair in front of the desk.

Taninè was Nicolò's wife, who cooked like an angel when she felt like it. Francesco was their only son.

"They're fine, thanks. Francesco's going to be taking his graduation exams this year."

Montalbano balked. Wasn't it just yesterday he had played cops and robbers with Francesco? And wasn't it just yesterday that Nicolò had red hair, whereas now it was suddenly all white?

"And how's your Livia doing?"

"She's fine, in good health."

Nicolò was too hip and wise to the facts of Montalbano's life to be satisfied by his diplomatic reply.

"Is anything wrong?"

"Well, let's say we're going through a period of crisis."

"At age fifty-six, you're having crises, Montalbà?" said his friend Zito, half ironic, half amused. "Don't make me laugh! By the time one reaches our age, there's no turning back."

The inspector decided it was best to get immediately to the point.

"I came—"

"—to talk about that girl who was killed, I figured that out right away, the moment you entered. What can I do for you?"

"You need to give me a hand."

"I'm at your service, as usual."

Montalbano pulled the two photographs out of his pocket and handed them to him.

"Nobody told us this morning that the girl had this tattoo," said Nicolò.

"Now you know. And you're the only journalist who does."

"It's a very artistic tattoo; the colors of the wings are beautiful," Zito commented. Then he asked, "You still haven't identified her?"

"No."

"Tell me what you want me to do."

"I want you to air these photos on the evening news and broadcast them again during the evening update and on the late-night edition. We want to know anyone who knew a girl slightly over twenty with this kind of tattoo. You can say that anonymous phone calls are also welcome. Naturally you should give out the telephone number for here."

"And why not the police station's?"

"Have you any idea of the kind of mess Catarella might create?"

"Can I say at least that you're handling the investigation?"

"Yes, at least until the commissioner takes it away from me."

As he was heading back down to Vigàta, he noticed the beginnings of what promised to be one of those sunsets so beautiful as to seem fake or from a picture postcard.

It seemed best to head home to Marinella and enjoy it from the veranda, rather than to go back to the office. And hadn't the angler predicted that it would rain for a week? He therefore had to take advantage of this last offering of the season.

But perhaps it was better to pass by headquarters, stick his head in to inform Catarella, and then cut out. It proved to be the utterly wrong decision.

"Ah Chief Chief! Iss Signora Picarella!"

"On the phone?"

"The phone? She's right here, Chief! She's waiting for you!"

"Tell her I just called and I'm not coming in to the office."

"I already tol' 'er that, Chief, all by m'self, but she said she's gonna stay here all night if she has to, till you decide to come back!"

Ugh, what a pain in the ass and then some!

"Okay, tell you what. I'm going to go into my office. Wait five minutes, then send her in."

The case of Arturo Picarella's kidnapping had begun a week earlier. A rich, fifty-year-old wholesaler in wood, Picarella had built himself a beautiful villa just outside of town, where he lived with his wife Ciccina, who was famous all over town for throwing furious fits of jealousy, even in public, at her husband, who was equally well-known for his insatiable hunger for women. Their only son, who was married, worked as a bank teller in Canicattì and kept his distance, coming to Vigàta barely once a month to visit.

One night, around one o'clock, husband and wife were woken up by some noise on the ground floor. At first they heard footsteps, and then a chair being knocked over. Surely some burglars had broken in.

Then, after ordering his wife not to get out of bed and getting all dressed up, sport coat and shoes included, Picarella armed himself with the revolver he kept in the drawer of his bedside table, went downstairs, and immediately started firing blindly, feeling perhaps empowered to do so by the recent law on self-defense.

Shortly thereafter, a terrified Signora Ciccina heard the front open and close again. At that point she got up, ran to the window, and saw her husband, hands in the air, being forced into his own car by a masked man pointing a gun at him.

The car drove off, and Arturo Picarella had been missing ever since.

Such were the facts as recounted by an agitated Signora Ciccina.

It should be added that, along with Picarella, some five hundred thousand euros had also disappeared, withdrawn by the wood merchant from his bank the very day before, supposedly to close a deal about which nobody knew anything.

Ever since that moment, not a morning or evening went by without Signora Picarella coming to the station to ask, each time more angrily, if they had any news of her husband. The kidnapper had never come forth to demand a ransom, and Picarella's car had not been found.

Once Mimì Augello and Fazio were assigned the case, however, they immediately formed a precise and very different opinion of how the kidnapping had gone.

It took them one glance to ascertain that Picarella had made sure to empty the entire cartridge into the ceiling, which looked worse than a colander. Meanwhile the burglar, apparently unarmed since he hadn't returned fire, didn't flee, but somehow managed to react and take possession of the firearm.

The front door, moreover, turned out not to have been forced, nor had the safe that was hidden behind a big photograph of Great-Grandfather Filippo Picarella, founder of the dynasty.

And why hadn't the thief taken the three thousand euros that Signora Ciccina had left out on a side table, which her husband had given her that evening to pay a supplier the following day? And why hadn't he grabbed the solid-gold snuffbox that had belonged to the great-grandfather and lay right there, for all to see, on top of the three thousand euros, holding them down?

And why, also, did Arturo Picarella—who, according to his wife's statements, had been sleeping in T-shirt and underpants—get all dressed up very quickly before going downstairs to confront the burglar? By now, with their long-standing experience, Augello and Fazio took for granted that anyone who is woken up in the middle of the night by burglars normally gets straight out of bed and goes to confront the thieves however he may happen to be dressed, in pajamas, underwear, or naked. The wholesaler's manner of behavior was at the very least extremely odd, if not downright suspicious.

Augello and Fazio had submitted a report to their superior which came to a conclusion that could in no way be revealed to Signora Ciccina. A conclusion supported, moreover, by rumors circulating around town, according to which Arturo Picarella had lost his head over a stewardess he had met while flying back from Sweden, where he had gone to buy wood.

In short, the way Augello and Fazio saw it, Mr. Picarella, with the complicity of a friend, had staged a little scene, pretending to be kidnapped but in fact heading off for a few months to the Bahamas or the Maldives in the company of his lovely stewardess. Another detail not to be ignored: The passport of Arturo Picarella happened to be in the pocket of the sport coat he put on that fateful night.

"Inspector," Signora Ciccina began after she'd been shown in, clearly restraining herself from yelling. "I'm telling you this only to ease my conscience: You should know that I've filed a statement with the minister."

Montalbano understood not a thing.

"A statement with the minister?"

"Oh, yes."

"About what?"

"About you."

"About me? Why?"

"Because you are taking the disappearance of my poor husband very lightly!"

It took him a good hour to persuade her to return home. He swore to a pack of lies, saying that whole squads of policemen, some of them coming from afar, were scouring the countryside looking for Mr. Picarella.

So much for the sunset. When he got to Marinella, the sun had already long gone down. He flicked on the TV, tuned in to the Free Channel, and immediately saw the photograph of the dead girl's tattoo on the screen. Nicolò Zito was doing what he had asked him to do.

Montalbano watched the newscast to the end. Four hundred Third World refugees had come ashore from Lampedusa only to be sent on to concentration—well, "first reception" camps. A branch of the Banca Regionale was robbed by three armed men. A fire had broken out in a supermarket, a clear case of arson. Some poor homeless wretch living on alms was beaten within an inch of his life by five youths who had decided to kill a little time that way. A fourteen-year-old girl was raped by—

He changed the channel, switching to TeleVigàta. And there was Pippo Ragonese, the political editorialist with a face like a chicken's ass, speaking. The inspector was about to change the channel again when Ragonese mentioned his name.

". . . thanks to the well-known inertia—and there's no better way to define it, only worse—of Inspector Montalbano, we are certain that this new, horrendous crime discovered at the Salsetto will also remain unsolved. That poor girl's murderer can sleep peacefully. Also unsolved, to date, is the peculiar kidnapping of businessman Arturo Picarella. And in this regard I cannot refrain from bringing to the attention of our viewers that Mrs. Picarella has complained to us about the discourteous treatment, to say the least, she has received from the above-mentioned Inspector Montalbano—"

He turned it off and went to open the refrigerator. His heart leapt at the sight of four mullets prepared as God had intended, ready for frying. Pippo Ragonese could go take it you-know-where. Montalbano slid them from the plate into a skillet, which he set over a burner. Then, to avoid a repeat of the previous evening, when Livia's phone call had sent his meal to the dogs, he ran to unplug the telephone.

Seated outside on the veranda, he dispatched the mullets, which had come out well but not as crispy as Adelina was capable of making them. Since he still felt a little hungry, he searched the fridge and found half a dish of leftover caponata. Sniffing it carefully, he convinced himself it was all right, took it outside, and wolfed it down.

He plugged the phone back in. Then he wondered: *What if Livia had called and found no one at home?* Considering that seas were rough between them—with gale-force winds, in fact—Livia was liable to think that he had disconnected the phone precisely because he didn't want to hear from her. It was best if he called her first. He dialed her number at Boccadasse, but there was no answer. And so he tried her cell phone.

"The telephone of the person you are trying to reach may be turned off or—"

Maybe she'd gone to the movies and would check in later.

He sat back down on the veranda to smoke a cigarette.

Unfortunately my relationship with Livia has reached a cross-roads, and I must absolutely make a choice, he thought, feeling himself overwhelmed by a wave of melancholy that immediately made his eyes glisten.

It took a great deal of courage to throw away years and years of love, trust, complicity. What he had with Livia was an out-and-out marriage, even if not sanctioned by the law or the Church. He felt like laughing whenever he heard bishops and cardinals make public proclamations against recognizing common-law marriage. How many marriages celebrated with the requisite priest and regalia had he seen last much less time than his arrangement with Livia?

On the other hand, maybe it took even greater courage to carry on in the situation they found themselves in now.

One thing was certain: They needed a clarification, of the ferocious, mutually flaying kind that draws blood. But that sort of clarification couldn't be made over the phone; the voice alone wouldn't suffice. Their two bodies also had to take part. One look would have told far more than a hundred words.

The telephone rang. He looked at his watch. It was eleven in the evening, and it must surely be Livia. As he was going to pick up, he was thinking he would suggest that she come down to Vigàta on the following Saturday.

"Inspector Montalbano?" said an old man's voice he didn't recognize at first.

"Yes, who's this?"

"Headmaster Burgio."

Good God, how long had it been since he'd heard from him! After the headmaster's wife died, Burgio had moved to Fela, to the home of a daughter of his, a teacher.

How old was he these days? Ninety?

"Forgive me for calling so late," said Burgio.

"Not at all! How are you?"

"I get by. I'm calling you because I saw the tattoo of the poor murdered girl on the Free Channel."

"Did you recognize her?"

"No, I phoned you about the butterfly tattoo."

"I didn't know you were an expert on butterflies."

"I'm not, in fact, but my son-in-law is. I called you up so late because tomorrow morning he's leaving and will be away for a week. If you don't mind, I'll put him on for you."

"By all means. Thanks."

"Hello, this is Gaspare Leontini," said Burgio's son-in-law. "Since I've got a little butterfly collection—I'm just an amateur, mind you . . ."

Those words set Montalbano's mind wandering. Once

upon a time, at least according to nineteenth-century novels, a butterfly collection was a profitable possession to have, in that it was an excellent pretext for luring a pretty girl to one's bedroom.

"Come and see my butterfly collection," the mustachioed seducers in knickers would say, and the girls would take the bait, or pretend to take the bait, and inevitably end up pinned like butterflies. After that, pretty girls grew a little wiser, and if a man didn't have a nice collection of checkbooks . . .

"Hello, are you still there?" asked Leontini.

"Of course, of course. Go on."

"Well, when I saw that image on television, I said to my father-in-law that perhaps I could . . . but maybe you already know everything."

He needed a little encouragement, did Signor Leontini.

"I don't know anything at all, I assure you."

"All right, then. That butterfly is a sphinx."

O matre santa, *what's a sphinx got to do with butterflies? Wasn't the sphinx in Egypt?* This was all he needed.

"A sphinx in what sense, if I may ask?"

"A sphinx moth, actually. The *Sphingidae* are a particular family of moth. There are another one hundred and eighty thousand known species of *Lepidoptera*, but generally they are divided into two subspecies: the *homoneura*, the main family of which are the *hepialidae*, and the *heteroneura*—"

"Is it a sexual difference?" asked Montalbano, utterly confused.

"I don't understand," said Leontini.

"Well, since you said '*homo-neura*' and '*hetero-neura*,' I thought that—"

"It has nothing to do with sex."

"I'm sorry."

"And the *heteroneura* include the families of the *Tine-idae, Tortricidae, Alucitidae, Pyralidae* . . ."—And what about the *Atridae?*—". . . those, in short, known as *microlepidoptera*, which also include common nocturnal moths . . ."

Montalbano rebelled, refusing to have any truck with common nocturnal moths.

"Listen, Signor Leontini, could we get back to the sphinx?"

"Of course, sorry for digressing. The sphingids are characterized by a fat hairy body and the fact that their hind wings are smaller than the forewings."

"How many wings does a moth usually have?"

Leontini hesitated before answering. He must certainly have been wondering how there could be people on earth who had never taken a good look at a moth or a butterfly in their lives.

"Four."

The inspector had never noticed this, and he felt a little embarrassed.

"The sphingids are migratory," Leontini continued.

"Migratory? Don't they have very short lives?"

"The species is capable of crossing an entire ocean."

"What do you mean?"

"It's true, though many people don't know it. During migration, they fly in a straight line, and once they've reached their destination, they resume flying in their more typical manner, in short, broken lines, as if uncertain and confused. And of course they're nocturnal, as I'm sure you've seen."

He never even saw butterflies on spring mornings.

"Tell me, Signor Leontini, do they have a country of origin or preference?"

"Well, most moths and butterflies are nonmigratory. To

give you a few examples, in Peru you'll find *Catopsilia argante*, in Colombia *Morpho cypris*, in the Moluccas you've got *Papilio deiphontes*, or, again in Peru, *Lycorea cleobaea*, or . . ."

Matre santa, the floodgates had opened!

"And where does one find the sphingids?"

"Those moths are happy just about anywhere, so long as there are potato fields nearby."

"Why's that?"

"Because their larvae live on potatoes."

The inspector thanked Leontini, thanked Burgio, too, and hung up.

By now he could have written a C+ term paper, at the very least, on *Lepidoptera*. But not one new line on the investigation. The phone call had been as useless as it was long. He had wanted to know if the image of that particular moth might actually mean something, but the answer was no. Maybe the girl had chosen it at random, perhaps flipping through the pages of a catalogue.

After spending an hour on the veranda, smoking and watching the faraway lights of a pair of boats, it was clear that Livia wasn't going to call, and so he went to bed.

Before he fell asleep, a sudden, painful thought flashed through his mind.

The love between him and Livia had been exactly like the flight of a sphinx moth.

At first, and for many years, it had been straight, sure, focused, and determined, capable of spanning an entire ocean.

Then, at a certain point, that splendid, straight line of flight had broken apart, zigzagging this way and that. It became—how had Leontini put it?—uncertain and confused.

The thought tormented him, ruining his night's sleep.

4

In the station's parking lot he pulled up alongside a Ferrari. Who could it belong to? Surely to a cretin, whatever the actual name on the registration.

For only a cretin could tool around town in a car like that. Then there was a second category, the imbeciles, closely related to cretins with Ferraris, made up of people who, to go shopping, needed to climb into an SUV with four-wheel drive, fourteen lamps between headlights, road lights and fog lights, shovels and pickaxes, emergency ladder, compass, and special windshield wipers for eventual sandstorms. And what about the latest maniacs, the ones with the Hummers?

"Ahh Chief!" Catarella exclaimed. "There's summon 'ere waitin' for yiz since nine 'cause he wants a talk to ya poissonally in poisson."

"Does he have an appointment?"

"No, sir. But 'e says iss important. 'Is name is . . ." He stopped and looked down at a scrap of paper. "'E writ it down for me 'ere. 'Is name is De Dodo."

Was it possible? Like the extinct flightless bird?

"You sure that's his name, Cat?"

"Cross my heart, Chief. Then there'd be two phone calls from two people who was lookin'—"

"You can tell me about it later."

Naturally, the fortyish man who came into his office had a different name from the one written down and cited by Catarella: Francesco Di Noto. Decked out in Armani, top-of-the-line loafers worn without socks, Rolex, shirt open to a golden crucifix suffocating in a forest of unkempt, rampant black hair.

He was surely the idiot tooling around in the Ferrari. But the inspector wanted confirmation.

"My compliments on your beautiful car."

"Thanks. It's a 360 Modena. I've also got a Porsche Carrera."

Double cretin with fireworks.

"What can I do for you?"

"Actually *I* was hoping to do something for *you*."

Double cretin with fireworks, and cocky to boot.

"Oh, yeah? What?"

"I got back from Cuba day before yesterday after spending a month there. I go there often."

"On vacation or because you're a Communist?"

The other gave him a bewildered look and then started laughing.

"What did I say that was so funny?"

"Me, a Communist? With a Ferrari and a Porsche? . . . Can you really imagine me as a Communist?"

"Actually, Mr. Di Noto, I can. And how. Precisely *because* you have two cars like yours, wear Armani, and own a Rolex . . . But let's drop it, shall we? It's better that way. So you go to Cuba for cultural reasons?"

He was purposely trying to provoke him, but the guy didn't even realize it.

"I go to Cuba because I have three girlfriends there!"

"Three? All at the same time?"

"Yes. But none of them knows about the others, naturally."

"Naturally. But tell me something, just out of personal curiosity: How many have you got here?"

Di Noto laughed.

"Here I've got a wife and a two-year-old son. And it was my father-in-law who put up the capital to start my own company, you know what I mean? Here I can't mess around; I gotta play it straight."

I hope your wife also has three boyfriends, Montalbano thought, *without you knowing about it, naturally.*

But he didn't voice his thought and merely said:

"Sorry, but what line of business is your company in?"

"Fish export."

So that was why the price of fish had become so stratospheric! To pay for this asshole's cars and girlfriends!

"You were telling me about Cuba."

"Right. My very last evening in Havana, which is to say, three days ago, I went with Myra, one of my three girlfriends, to a nightclub. All at once I saw a guy come in and sit down at the table next to ours, accompanied by a really fine-looking blonde. He was completely drunk and looked familiar to me. And, in fact, after staring at him for a while, I realized who he was."

"And who was he?"

"Arturo Picarella."

Montalbano jumped out of his chair.

"Are you sure?"

"Absolutely sure. I didn't know a thing about what had happened to him, but yesterday my wife told me he was kidnapped and never heard from again. My jaw dropped, but I didn't say anything to my wife. I wanted to come here first to find out what I should do."

"You did the right thing. Listen, Mr. Di Noto, had you

been anywhere else before you went to the establishment where you think you saw Picarella?"

"Of course. From seven to nine o'clock, I was at Anya's— we'll call her my oldest girlfriend—then from nine-thirty to eleven I was at Tanya's—we'll call her my middle girlfriend— and then from midnight to two, at Myra's—"

"—and we'll call her—" said Montalbano.

"—my new girlfriend."

"I see. So at what time did you go to that nightclub?"

"About two-thirty in the morning."

"Naturally, you'd had something to drink at your various girlfriends' places?"

"Of course. I see what you're getting at. No, sir, I wasn't drunk. The man I saw was most definitely Arturo Picarella. I've been playing with him at the club for years."

"So why didn't you go up to him to say hello?"

"Are you kidding? It might have put him in an awkward position."

"Your testimony, Mr. Di Noto, is certainly an important one. But it's not enough to—"

"Have a look at this," the other interrupted him.

He pulled a photograph out of his jacket pocket and handed it to Montalbano.

It showed Di Noto kissing a girl. But the photographer had also captured part of the table next to them. The face of the man whose ear was being licked by a blonde was undoubtedly the missing Picarella, whom Montalbano had seen again and again in the dozens of photographs brought to him by Signora Ciccina.

So Augello and Fazio had been wrong as to the country to which the man had fled to live it up in style with his lover. It was Cuba, not the Maldives or the Bahamas.

"Can you leave me this photo?"

"That's easier said than done."

"Why?"

"My good inspector, I would gladly let you have it, but if you then use it, and the photo appears on TV and my wife sees it, do you realize the trouble I'm gonna be in?"

"I promise I'll arrange it so that you'll be entirely unrecognizable in the photo."

"I'm in your hands, Inspector."

As soon as the Ferrari drove off with a roar that shook even the floor of the office, the inspector called Catarella.

"I want you to go to Montelusa to see your photographer friend. What's his name again?"

"Cicco De Cicco, Chief."

"You're going to give him this photograph and tell him to print several copies of it after changing the features on this gentlemen here, the one kissing the girl. But be careful: only him. I mean it. Not the other man. Now go."

"Atcher service, Chief. But could you 'splain sumpin a me?"

"Sure."

"Does 'features' mean 'face'?"

"Very good."

"Tanks. I'll git Galluzzo to manna phones. Ah, an' I wannit a say that two people called about the buttafly."

"Are we supposed to call them back or will they call us back?"

Catarella looked dumbfounded.

"They din't say nuttin."

"But did they leave a phone number?"

"Yessir. I writ it down on this piece a paper."

He handed it to Montalbano.

"All right, then, go, but send me Galluzzo before he sits down at the switchboard."

On the piece of paper were the names of a certain Signor Gracezza and a certain Signora Appuntata, each followed by a number in which it was impossible to tell the fives from the sixes and the threes from the eights.

He handed the piece of paper to Galluzzo.

"See if you can figure these numbers out. Call the man first, and the woman after."

While he was waiting, he decided to give Pasquano a ring.

It was barely ten o'clock, but the doctor normally began performing his autopsies around five in the morning.

"Montalbano here. The doctor in?"

"As far as that goes, yes, he's in."

It wasn't an encouraging answer.

"Could you have him come to the phone a minute?"

"You must be kidding."

"This is Inspector Montalbano. Please call him for me."

"Inspector, I recognized your voice right away, but to be honest with you, I'm just not up to it. The doctor's in a really nasty mood today, believe me."

"Do you know if he's done the autopsy on the girl we found yesterday?"

"Yes, he has."

"All right, then, thanks."

The only solution was to go in person, at the risk of being buried in obscenities by Pasquano and having to dodge a flying scalpel or a few dead body parts.

The telephone rang.

"Inspector, I've got Signor Graceffa on the line. That's his real name, not the way Catarella wrote it. I'll put him through."

"Mr. Graceffa? This is Inspector Montalbano. Did you ask for me this morning?"

"Yes. Last night I phoned the Free Channel and Mr. Zito told me to call you."

"Thanks for calling. What do you have to tell me?"

Silence.

"Hello?"

Nothing.

Matre santa, what had happened? Had the line gone dead? For some mysterious reason, whenever the line went dead as Montalbano was talking, he broke out into a cold sweat and felt like a little boy who had suddenly been orphaned.

"Hello? Hello?" the inspector started yelling.

"I'm here."

"So why don't you speak?"

"Iss a delicate matter."

"Would you rather not discuss it over the phone?"

"No, because any minute now, my niece Concetta's gonna come back from doing the shopping."

"I see. Could you come here?"

"Not before noon."

"All right, I'll be waiting for you."

"May I?" asked Augello from the doorway.

"Come in and sit down, Mimì. Did Salvo let you sleep last night?"

"Luckily, yes. But I came in late because Beba had to go to the doctor's, and so I had look after the kid."

"What's wrong with Beba?"

"Woman stuff. Any news?"

"Nothing substantial. But soon there may be a bit of news, though it concerns a different case."

"Which one?"

"I'll tell you later."

He didn't want to set off the bomb about the sighting of Picarella until Catarella brought back the photo and Fazio was also there.

"Did you see that I asked Zito on the Free Channel to—"

"Yeah, I saw."

"After the broadcast, a certain Mr. Graceffa called and said he's coming by in the early afternoon. Some lady also called—"

The phone rang.

"Chief, there's a lady named Annunziata, not Appuntata."

"Put her on."

"Perhaps I wasn't clear enough, Inspector. She's here in person."

"Then show her into Inspector Augello's office."

Mimì gave him a questioning look.

"You listen to what she has to say, Mimì. She saw the broadcast and maybe can help us identify the girl."

"And where are you going?"

"I'm going to see Pasquano."

───

"Look, I'm warning you, this morning my cojones are smoking," was the doctor's courteous admonition the moment he saw the inspector.

Montalbano was not impressed and answered in kind. Pasquano became tractable only when one stood up to him.

"And you know what mine are like today? A steam engine."

"What the heck do you want?"

He had said "heck." Not "fuck," not "hell." Which meant he was really enraged.

"What's wrong, Doctor?"

"What's wrong is that last night, at the club, I had a straight flush."

"That's good, no?"

"No, because some son of a bitch also had a straight flush. Royal. You understand?"

"Perfectly, Doctor. Did you raise him?"

"Wouldn't you?"

"I don't gamble. You'll see, tonight you'll get another chance."

"Did you come here to console me?"

"I came to—"

"—to talk about the lives of *Phoenicopteri*?"

"No, if anything, about *Lepidoptera*."

"You mean the girl with the butterfly?"

"I do. And it's a moth."

"Look, she was definitely under thirty. About twenty-five, I'd say. She was killed by a single gunshot to the face, fired from about ten yards away."

"So the killer was a good shot?"

"Either a good shot or lucky."

"The science lab says it was a large-caliber weapon."

"You don't need all their science to know that. You only need to take a look at the damage it did. To give you an example, after grazing the left jawbone the bullet blew away half of her upper teeth, which were missing from the body."

"When was she killed?"

"The murder definitely took place during the night between Saturday and Sunday. Then, the following night, the killer got rid of the body by throwing it into the dump."

"But why would he hang on to it for all of Sunday?"

"That's not my concern. It's yours."

"Listen, Doctor, were you able to tell if she'd had sexual relations before being killed?"

"If she had, I would have told you already. And I especially would have told Prosecutor Tommaseo, which would have made him very happy."

"Was she a prostitute?"

"I would also rule that out."

"Why?"

"Because."

"What, in your opinion, was she doing at the moment she was shot?"

"Go ask the lady with the crystal ball."

"Let me rephrase that. Was she standing? Lying down? Sitting?"

"Definitely standing. And the person who shot her was behind her."

"Behind? Didn't he shoot her in the face?"

"In my opinion the girl turned around to look behind her at the very moment the killer pulled the trigger. Maybe the killer called to her, she turned around, and he shot her."

Montalbano thought about this for a moment.

"Hurry up with your excogitations," said the doctor. "I haven't got all this time to waste."

"Could the girl have been trying to escape?"

"Very likely, yes."

"Perhaps from an attempted rape?"

"For that hypothesis you'll have to check with Prosecutor Tommaseo."

Pasquano was really surly today.

"Where there any signs of rings on the fingers?"

"She wore one on her left pinkie, not the ring finger. Therefore she wasn't married. Or perhaps married according to another rite. Or maybe she was married and simply didn't wear a wedding ring."

"Any piercing?"

"None."

"What about the bites on her thigh?"

"Ah, those? Rats as big as puppy dogs."

"Is that all you can tell me, Doctor?"

"No."

"Look, Doctor, I haven't got time to waste, either."

"I found two things."

"Do you plan to tell me in monthly installments?"

"I found two little pieces of black wool inside her head."

"What does that mean?"

"What do you think it means? That those pieces of wool were congenital?"

"Maybe it means the bullet passed through something woolen before entering her flesh?"

"You can drop the 'maybe.'"

"She might have been wearing a turtleneck sweater."

"Here you can put back the 'maybe.'"

"And the second thing?"

"The second thing is that I found a little bit of purpurin under the fingernails of both hands."

"Purpurin?"

"For heaven's sake, don't repeat what I say, because it makes my balls spin even worse. You heard right: purpurin. Don't you know what purpurin is?"

"Isn't it a powder used in gilding?"

"Very good. You've passed the test with flying colors. Now get the hell out of here."

"One last question. Did she have any illnesses?"

"She'd been operated for appendicitis."

"No, I wanted to know if she had any illness for which she had to take medication."

"I get it. You're hoping you can identify her by going 'round to all the pharmacies in Vigàta and Montelusa. Sorry to disappoint you. The girl was in good health. And then some."

"What do you mean?"

"She had the body of an athlete."

"Or dancer?"

"Why not? And now, how do I have to tell you to get the fuck out of here?"

"Thank you for your exquisite courtesy, Doctor. I hope you get a royal full house tonight."

"Against four aces? You really are a bastard."

5

As he headed back down to Vigàta, it occurred to him that a bullet entering above the jawbone could not have passed through a turtleneck sweater. The trajectory would not allow it. It would be as if the bullet, after grazing the upper part of the collar, had suddenly climbed up a little ladder.

On the other hand, the girl might indeed have been wearing a black scarf wrapped up high, almost far enough to cover her mouth, as one does on certain particularly cold days. In that case, a few threads of wool could have been carried into the wound.

But this hypothesis didn't hold water, either, since the weather decidedly was not the kind in which one wore wool scarves. Not in Vigàta and environs, at least. Perhaps the girl had put on a scarf for a special occasion. And on what sort of special occasions does one wear a wool scarf? He couldn't think of any.

And then: Where can one dirty one's hands with purpurin?

And why was the purpurin under the girl's fingernails and not on her fingertips, as would have been more logical?

Before he entered Vigàta, the deluge the fisherman had forecast the previous day came pouring down.

He got drenched just walking from the parking lot to the main entrance of the police station.

"Mr. Beniamino Graceffa is here," Galluzzo informed the inspector as he was shaking the water off of his suit.

"Give me a minute to dry my hair, and then send him in."

In his office he opened up a file cabinet in which he kept a towel. He rubbed his head with this, then combed his hair. The water that had entered between his shirt and his skin bothered him, however. So he took off his shirt and dried his back, but the moment he put the wet shirt back on, it bothered him even more.

He started cursing the saints. He took his shirt off again and started waving it in the air. At that moment Mimì Augello walked in.

"You practicing for the bullfights?"

"Leave me alone. What did Signora Annunziata say?"

"A load of crap."

"Meaning?"

"She's afraid they're gonna kill her daughter Michela, too, who's eighteen. She showed me a photograph of her, a real jewel, Salvo."

"Why's she afraid her daughter will be killed?"

"Because Michela's also got a tattoo of a butterfly."

"The same one as the murdered girl?"

"No. She described it to me, and it's not the same at all. And hers is tattooed on her left tit."

"So what did you say to her?"

"First, that if the killers murdered all the girls with butter-fly tattoos, it would be a catacomb, as Catarella would say. And, second, to bring her daughter here, so I can carefully examine her tattoo."

"Have you gone insane?"

"I was just kidding, Salvo! You know something? You used to have a sense of humor."

"Well, with you, the minute there's a woman involved, one never knows if you're kidding or not."

"You know what I say? It's better if I leave. Bye, see you after lunch."

In the doorway appeared a short, rotund man of about seventy with a face so red it looked like a ripe tomato, and beady eyes buried in all the fat.

"May I come in?"

"Please do."

The man entered, and Montalbano gestured to him to sit down.

"Beniamino Graceffa's the name."

He sat down on the edge of a chair.

"I'm retired," he declared right off the bat, without the inspector having yet asked him anything.

"I'm seventy-two," he added, after a pause.

He sighed.

"And I've been a widower for ten years."

Montalbano let him talk.

"I got no children."

The inspector cast him a glance of encouragement.

"I'm looked after by Concetta, one of my sister Carmela's daughters."

Pause.

"Last night I was watching television."

Long pause. Montalbano figured it was perhaps his turn now.

"Did you recognize the tattoo?"

"Exactly the same."

"Where did you see it?"

53

Beniamino Graceffa's beady eyes sparkled. He licked his lips with the tip of his tongue.

"Where do you think I saw it, Inspector?" He gave a little smile and continued. "Behind a girl's shoulder."

"Was it in the same place? Near the left shoulder blade?"

"In the exact same place."

"And where was the girl when you saw the tattoo?"

"Iss a delicate matter."

"You've already said that, Mr. Graceffa."

"Lemme explain. About five months ago, my niece Concetta told me she couldn't come help me anymore for a while, seeing as how she had to go to Catania for a temporary job."

"And so?"

"And so my sister Carmela, who's afraid to leave me by myself, seeing as how I've had two heart attacks, found me a girl, a . . . how do you call 'em these days?"

"Home care assistant."

"Right. Actually my sister would have preferred an elderly person, but she didn't find any. And so she brought this Russian girl named Katya to my house."

"Very young?"

"Twenty-three years old."

"Pretty?"

Beniamino Graceffa brought the thumb, forefinger, and middle finger of his right hand to his lips and made the sound of a kiss. That said it all.

"Did she sleep at your place?"

"Of course." He stopped and looked around himself.

"Don't worry, there's just me and you here."

Graceffa leaned forward, towards the inspector.

"I'm still a man, you know."

"My compliments. Are you trying to tell me that you had relations with this girl?"

Graceffa made a disconsolate face.

"No way, Inspector! It wasn't possible!"

"Why not?"

"Inspector, one night when I couldn't stand it any longer, I went into her room. But there was nothing doing. I couldn't convince her, not even when I told her I was willing to spend a lot of money."

"What did you do then?"

"Inspector, I'm an old-fashioned gentleman, you know! What was I supposed to do? I let it drop."

"So how were you able to see the tattoo?"

"Inspector, can we talk man to man?"

"Of course."

"I saw that butterfly three or four times when the girl was taking a bath."

"Let me get this straight: You were with the girl when she was taking a bath?"

"No, Inspector, sir. She was alone in the bathroom, and I was outside."

"So how did you . . ."

"I was spying on her."

"From where?"

"Through the hole."

"The keyhole?"

"No, sir, you couldn't see anything through the keyhole, 'cause usually the key was in it and blocked the view."

"And so?"

"One day, when Katya went out shopping, I took my drill and enlarged a hole that was already there in the door."

Truly an old-fashioned gentleman.

"And the girl didn't notice?"

"It's a very old door."

"And was this girl blond or brunette?"

"Hair was black as ink."

"Well, the girl who was killed was blond."

"So much the better. I'm glad it wasn't her. Because a man can grow fond of a girl like that."

"How long was she at your place?"

"One month and twenty-four and a half days."

Surely he'd been counting, down to the minutes.

"Why did she leave?"

Graceffa sighed.

"My niece Concetta came back."

"Do you know how long the girl had been in Italy?"

"More than a year."

"What did she do before working for you?"

"She was a dancer in nightclubs in Salerno and Grosseto."

"Where was she from?"

"You mean the name of the town in Russia? She told me once, but I forget. If it comes back to me, I'll give you a call."

"But didn't she earn more working as a dancer in nightclubs?"

"She told me she earned a pittance as a home assistant."

"She never told you why she stopped working as a dancer?"

"She told me once that it wasn't her own choice, and that it was better for her to stay away for a while."

"Did she speak good Italian?"

"Good enough."

"Did she receive any visits from anyone during the time she lived with you?"

"Never."

"Did she get any days off?"

"Thursdays. But she was always back by ten o'clock in the evening."

"Did she often receive or make phone calls?"

"She had her own cell phone."

"Did it ring often?"

"During the day, at least ten times. At night I couldn't say."

"Man to man, Mr. Graceffa, did you ever happen to get up in the middle of the night and go listen at the girl's bedroom door?"

"Well, yeah. A few times."

"Did you hear her talking?"

"Yes, but she was talking too softly for me to understand anything. However . . ."

"Go on."

"Once, when her phone was discharged, she asked me if she could make a call on mine. I could hear her but I couldn't understand anything because she was speaking Russian. But she must have been talking to a girl because she kept calling her Sonya."

"Thank you, Mr. Graceffa. If you remember the name of the girl's town, give me a ring. I mean it."

It was already past lunchtime, and still no sign of Catarella.

The inspector decided to go to Enzo's. It was still raining.

He smoked a cigarette in the doorway, waiting for the water pouring down from the heavens to let up. Then he made a dash to his car, got in, and drove off. Luckily he found a parking spot close to the restaurant entrance.

"Inspector, I should warn you that the sea is really rough today," said Enzo by way of greeting.

"What the hell do I care? I don't have to go out on a boat."

"You're wrong. You should care, and how!"

"What do you mean?"

"Inspector, if the sea is rough, the fishing boats don't go out to fish, and therefore tomorrow, instead of fresh fish, you'll find a plate of frozen fish or a nice piece of *vitella alla milanese* under your nose."

Montalbano shuddered at the thought of *vitella alla milanese.*

"But is there any fish today?"

"Yes there is. Fresh as can be."

"So why frighten me in advance?"

Perhaps because he knew there wouldn't be any fresh fish the next day, he ordered a double serving of mullets.

When he stepped out of the trattoria, it was coming down in buckets. A walk along the jetty was out of the question. All he could do was go back to the station.

Still at the switchboard was Galluzzo.

"Any news of Catarella?"

"None."

"Anyone call for me?"

"Zito the newsman. Says to call him back."

"All right, ring him up and put it through to my desk."

He didn't have time to finish drying his head before the phone rang.

"Salvo? This is Nicolò. Did you see it?"

"No. See what?"

"I broadcast the photos of the tattoo on the morning edition at ten and on the afternoon edition at one."

"Thanks. I've even spoken with the two people who called you."

"Did they tell you anything useful?"

"One of them, Graceffa, maybe yes. You should—"

"—keep broadcasting the pictures. I got that. Whatever you say."

Finally, just a few minutes before four, Catarella returned in glory and triumph.

"Iss all done, Chief! Cicco de Cicco wasted a lotta time, but 'e did a maspertiece!"

He pulled four photographs out of an envelope and set them down on the inspector's desk.

"Look atta 'riginal, then look atta tree copies 'n' see how the man you wanted changed is changed!"

Indeed, Di Noto, now with a mustache and glasses and a few white hairs, looked like quite another person.

"Thanks, Cat, and give Cicco de Cicco my compliments. When Inspector Augello and Fazio return, tell them to come into my office."

Catarella walked out strutting like a peacock. Montalbano paused to think for a minute, then made up his mind and slipped the original and three copies into a drawer.

Fazio and Augello arrived almost simultaneously at around four-fifteen.

"Catarella said you wanted to see us," said Mimì.

"Yes. Sit down, both of you, and listen to what I have to say."

He told them what he'd found out from Dr. Pasquano and what Graceffa had said to him.

"What do you think?"

"I'm wondering," Mimì led off, "if there's any signifi-cance in the fact that two girls of more or less the same age, probably both foreign, had the same tattoo in the same place."

"But, Mimì, you yourself told me that nowadays girls have tattoos all over their bodies!"

"Of the same moth?"

"What makes you so sure it's the same?"

"It's what Graceffa told you."

"Yes, but bear in mind that Graceffa is over seventy, he was spying on the girl through a hole and from a certain distance, and one can just imagine how closely he was studying her left shoulder blade when the girl was naked in front of him. Then tell me how reliable you think his testimony really is!"

"It's possible that seeing all that divine grace before his eyes, Graceffa's vision became more keen," Augello retorted.

"I, on the other hand, have been thinking about the purpurin," said Fazio.

"Good for you," said Montalbano.

"Where is it that people work with purpurin?" Fazio wondered aloud, then answered his own question: "At furniture factories."

"Do people still make gilded furniture?" Montalbano asked.

"Of course they do!" said Augello. "The other day I went to the wedding of a distant relative of Beba's. Well, the furniture was all—"

"At restoration workshops," said Montalbano.

"No, it wasn't," said Augello, flustered. "Why do you say that? The furniture was not in restoration workshops, it was all in the house."

"Mimì, what I meant was that one could also find purpurin in the workshop of someone who restores antique furniture."

"I'll start having a look around tomorrow," said Fazio.

"All right, but you can't limit yourself to Vigàta. You have to look in Montelusa as well, and in some of the neighboring towns. The dump at the Salsetto is used by people from Vigàta, Montelusa, Giardina, Gallotta . . ."

"And sometimes even by people from Borgina," said Augello.

"Would to God we discovered that the murder occurred in Borgina!" Montalbano exclaimed.

"Why?"

"Have you forgotten that Borgina falls within the jurisdiction of Licata? In that case the investigation would be turned over to them."

"I was thinking about the purpurin," said Fazio.

"You've already said that."

"Chief, I was wondering why the purpurin was under her fingernails but not on her fingers."

"I was wondering the same thing."

"But I saw the body and you didn't. And I had the impression . . ."

"Of what?"

"That the girl had been stripped naked and washed after she was killed," Mimì cut in. "I had the same thought as Fazio."

"She was carefully washed, but whoever did it forgot to clean the fingernails," said Fazio.

"Excuse me, but why do you both think she'd been washed?"

"Because there was no trace of blood on her neck," said Mimì.

"Not a drop," confirmed Fazio.

"Which means that if she hadn't been washed, we might be able to determine where she was killed?"

"Probably, yes," the two said in chorus.

The telephone rang. Fazio and Augello made as if to rise and leave the room.

"Wait, I have something else to tell you."

"Chief, there's a lady onna line an' I canna 'nerstand 'er name."

"Try telling me what you think it is."

"Cirrinciò, Chief."

"Actually, you got it right, Cat. Put her on."

The inspector got worried. Want to bet Adelina was going to tell him she couldn't come to clean house and prepare dinner?

"What is it, Adelì?"

"Signore, you gotta 'scuse me but I gotta tell you my boy Pasquali, when I went to see 'im in prison this morning, he said he wanna talk to you."

"They haven't yet granted him house arrest?"

"Not yet, signore."

"Are you coming tomorrow?"

"Of course, signore."

"When you prepare the food, don't forget that there's not going to be any fresh fish at the market tomorrow."

"Leave it to me."

With the threat of *vitella alla milanese* dispelled, he felt cheered up.

He leaned back in his chair and, wanting to amuse himself with a bit of playacting, he looked very seriously at the other two.

6

So seriously that Augello got worried.

"What is it?"

"I've got some big news about the Picarella kidnapping."

"News?" asked Fazio, wonderstruck.

Mimì instead took a mocking tone.

"You're not going to tell me they've asked for a ransom!"

"Does this seem like a laughing matter to you?"

"Absolutely, because I don't believe for a minute that he was kidnapped!"

"What about you, Fazio? If I told you that Signora Ciccina had been called by the kidnappers demanding ransom, would you believe it or not?"

"I could believe it if—" Fazio began, but Mimì got angry and interrupted him.

"But we both arrived at the same conclusion, you and I! How is it you've suddenly changed your mind?"

"Please let me speak, Inspector Augello. I could believe it if I thought Picarella had spent all the money he took from his safe, and had put his friend up to phoning for more."

"Then I'm with you!" said Mimì.

"So you two continue to believe that the kidnapping was staged?"

"Yes," said Augello and Fazio in unison.

Montalbano opened the drawer, grabbed a copy of the photo, and handed it to Mimì.

Fazio stood up and got behind Mimì to have a look himself.

"Holy shit!" exclaimed Augello.

"It's him!" said Fazio.

"When was this taken?" asked Mimì.

"How did you get this?" Fazio followed up.

"Calm down. The photo dates from no more than three or four days ago," said Montalbano.

"Where was it taken?" asked Mimì.

"In Havana, at a nightclub. See? You guys were wrong. Picarella was not in the Maldives or the Bahamas, but in Cuba."

"The son of a bitch!" said Mimì.

"How did you get this?" Fazio asked again.

"That man there with the mustache and glasses gave it to me. He's from Vigàta."

"I don't know 'im," said Fazio.

"Actually I think you do," said Montalbano, handing him the original photo.

"Why, that's Di Noto, the fish exporter!"

"Bravo. I had his features changed to keep him out of it."

"So what do we do now?"

"Simple. Tomorrow morning, when Fazio goes out looking for furniture works and restorers, you are going to summon Signora Ciccina Picarella and give her the lowdown."

"Yeah, and that lady, jealous as she is, is liable to take it out on me!"

"Risks of the profession, Mimì."

"But how should I proceed?"

"You have to handle her very tactfully, Mimì. Start, for example, by telling her that you are absolutely certain that her husband, wherever he is, is fine. Great, in fact. Actually, he couldn't possibly be better. And at that very moment, as the lady's worries are starting to fade, you show her the photograph."

"What if she asks me how we got hold of it?"

"You tell her it was sent to us anonymously."

"You know what I'm going to do? I'm going to call her right now and tell her to come here. That way I don't have to think about it. And then, if need be, I'll call you for help."

"Call me? I've got nothing to do with this case, Mimì, and I don't want to have anything to do with it. The honor of solving it lies with you and Fazio. So don't even try."

He stayed at the station another half an hour. Then, worried that Mimì, not knowing what to do with Signora Ciccina, might call him, he decided to leave.

"You goin' home, Chief?"

"Yeah, Cat. I'll see you in the morning."

The rain was taking a short break. But it was threatening to start again even harder than before.

Once he set off, he realized he didn't really feel like going home. With all the rain that had fallen, he wouldn't be able to sit out on the veranda. He would have to eat in the kitchen or in front of the television. Alone, in short, between four walls, rehashing his situation with Livia. Imagine the fun! What to do? Go to Enzo's, or try another trattoria? And what if it started deluging again?

Lost amidst these doubts, he was driving very slowly when somebody behind him honked. He pulled over to let them pass. But the car coming up behind him not only did not pass him, it gave another toot of the horn.

Were these people bent on breaking his balls?

It had started raining again, and, as a result, he could just barely see in the rearview mirror that the high-powered car behind him was green in color. He lowered his window, stuck out his arm, and motioned for the car to pass. The only reply was another honk.

Did they want to have it out? If so, they would get their wish.

He pulled over right there, at the side of the road. The car behind him did the same. Then the inspector lost patience. Despite the rain, he opened the car door and got out. At once he saw the driver of the other car open the door on the passenger's side.

He ran and jumped into the green car, ready to throw the first punch, but found himself in the arms of Ingrid, who was laughing.

"I really got you pissed off, didn't I, Salvo!"

Ingrid Sjostrom! His friend, confidante, and accomplice! He hadn't seen her for at least six months.

"What a wonderful surprise, Ingrid! Where were you going?"

"To meet a friend and go out to dinner with him. And where were you going?"

"Home to Marinella."

"Are you alone? Do you have any engagements?"

"I'm absolutely free."

"Wait a second."

She picked up her cell phone, which was lying on the dashboard, and dialed a number.

"Manlio? This is Ingrid. Listen, I'm sorry, but I have to tell you, as I was getting dressed to come to your place, I suddenly got a terrible migraine. Can we put it off till tomorrow? Okay? You're an angel."

She set down the cell phone.

"Never had a migraine in my life," she said.

"Where shall we go?" asked the inspector.

"To your place. If Adelina left you something to eat, we can share it."

"Okay."

With Ingrid there, the prospect of an evening at home changed.

"I'll go ahead and you follow."

"No, Salvo, my car is incapable of following behind yours. The engine suffers. Give me your house keys, I'll go on ahead."

When he got there, Ingrid was in the bedroom. She was rifling through her bag.

"Salvo, I'm going to take a shower. My clothes are all damp and sticky."

"When you're done I'm going to take one myself."

At that moment Ingrid's purse, which she had wanted to set down on the nightstand, fell to the floor, spilling its contents all over the room. They started picking things up, and after a while Ingrid checked to see if they'd found everything.

"Bah," she said, perplexed.

"What's missing?"

"I thought I had a packet of condoms, but I can't find it now. Maybe I didn't bring it."

Montalbano looked at her dumbfounded.

"Why are you making that face?"

"Isn't it up to the man to provide them?"

"Theoretically, yes. But if he forgets, then what do you do? Start singing, *Casta diva*?"

"Wait and I'll have a better look."

"Come on, Salvo. I don't need them. Especially since I've decided to spend the evening with you . . . ," she said, heading into the bathroom.

Especially since she's decided to spend the evening with me, she doesn't need any condoms, he repeated to himself. Was Montalbano the hypothetical satyr supposed to feel offended? Or was Montalbano the prude supposed to feel proud?

Lost in doubt, he went to open the French door to the veranda and stepped outside.

It was raining relentlessly, of course.

If the water from the heavens hadn't wet the table or bench it was because the overhanging roof had done its job. To make up for this, however, the sea was washing all the way up to the bottom of the veranda, having swallowed up the entire beach.

All things considered, he could set the table outside, even if it was a little chilly.

He opened the refrigerator and was disappointed. Except for some olives and tumazzo cheese, there was nothing. Want to bet they would be forced to go out and look for a place to eat? He opened the oven.

"O ye of little faith!" he reproached himself aloud.

Adelina had made *pasta 'ncasciata* and *melanzane alla parmigiana*. He only had to light the oven and reheat them a little.

Ingrid came out, wearing his bathrobe.

"You can go in now."

Montalbano didn't move, but kept looking at her.

"Well?"

"Ingrid, how long have we known each other?"

"Over ten years. Why?"

"How is it you've become even more beautiful?"

"Are you finally starting to get ideas?"

"No, it was a simple observation. Listen, I had a look outside and I think we can eat on the veranda."

"Good idea. I'll prepare everything myself. Go."

If the *pasta 'ncasciata*, when they had finished it off, was greatly missed, the *melanzane alla parmigiana*, when it reached its end, deserved some sort of long funeral lament. Meeting an honorable death along with the pasta was also a bottle of tender, beguiling white wine, while to the *melanzane* they sacrificed half a bottle of another white, which under a veneer of utter meekness concealed a treacherous soul.

"We must finish that bottle," said Ingrid.

Montalbano went and fetched the olives and tumazzo.

Afterwards, Ingrid cleared the table and Montalbano heard her starting to wash the dishes.

"You can leave them," he said. "Adelina's coming tomorrow."

"Sorry, Salvo, but I can't help myself."

The inspector got up, grabbed a brand-new bottle of whisky and two glasses, and went back out on the veranda.

A little while later, Ingrid sat down beside him. Montalbano filled her glass half full. They drank.

"Now we can talk," said Ingrid.

While stuffing themselves they hadn't spoken except to comment on what they were stuffing themselves with. During the frequent silences, the smell and sound of the sea splashing against the piles supporting the veranda became an extra seasoning and backdrop as unexpected as it was welcome.

"How's your husband doing?"

"Fine, I think."

"What do you mean, 'I think'?"

"Ever since he was elected to Parliament, he's been living in Rome, where he bought himself an apartment. He comes to Montelusa once a month but spends more time with his constituents than with me. Anyway, it's been years since we've had sexual relations."

"I see. Any lovers?"

"Just so I can feel alive. B-grade. They come and go."

They sat in silence a bit, listening to the sounds of the sea.

"Salvo, what's wrong?"

"With me? Nothing? What could be wrong?"

"I don't believe you. You're talking to me but you're thinking of something else."

"I'm sorry. I've got an important case on my hands and from time to time I get distracted thinking about it. It involves a girl who was—"

"I'm not going to take the bait."

"I don't understand."

"Salvo, you want to change the subject and so you're trying to arouse my curiosity. But I'm not going to take the bait. Mostly, you're incapable of lying; I've known you too long for that to work. What's wrong?"

"Nothing."

This time Ingrid filled the glasses. They drank.

"How's Livia?"

She'd gone directly on the attack.

"Fine, I think."

"I see. Do you feel like talking to me about it?"

"Maybe in a little while."

The air was so briny that it burned the skin and expanded the lungs.

"Do you feel cold?" the inspector asked.

"I feel perfectly fine."

She slipped her arm under his, squeezed it, and laid her head on his shoulder.

"... in short, not until late August did she finally deign to answer the phone when I called. Believe me, I must have called her every day for almost a month. I was starting to get seriously worried. Livia said she herself had also tried to call me several times from Massimiliano's boat, but there was no reception, given that they were out on the open sea. I didn't believe her."

"Why not?"

"What were they doing? Sailing around the world without ever going ashore? Is it possible they never entered a port equipped with a telephone? Come on! So, when we did finally get a chance to see each other, the shit hit the fan. When I think back on it now, I believe I was a little aggressive."

"Knowing you, I'd say it was a bit more than 'a little.'"

"All right, but it helped. She said there had been something between her and—"

"Her little cousin Massimiliano? No, you don't say!"

"That's what I feared, too. No, it was with some guy named Gianni, a friend of Massimiliano's who was with them on the boat. That was all she would tell me. Listen, Ingrid, in your opinion, what does that mean, that there was 'something'?"

"Do you really want to know?"

"Yes."

"When a woman says there's been something with a man, it means there's been everything."

"Ah."

He downed his glass, refilled it. Ingrid did likewise.

"Salvo, don't tell me that you're so naïve you didn't arrive at the same conclusion."

"No, I came to that conclusion at once. I just wanted you to confirm it for me. And so I threw down my ace."

"I don't understand."

"I told her I didn't exactly spend the summer twiddling my thumbs, either."

Ingrid gave a start.

"Is that true?"

"It's true."

"You?!"

"Me, unfortunately."

"So what did you do when you weren't twiddling your thumbs?"

"I met a girl much younger than me. Twenty-two years old. I really don't know how it could have happened."

"Did you do her?"

Montalbano felt a little put off by her manner of speech.

"It was a pretty serious thing for me. And I really suffered because of it."

"Okay, but between all the tears and regrets, you made love to her. Is that right?"

"Yes."

Ingrid embraced him, stood up slightly, then kissed him on the lips.

"Welcome to the sinners' club, asshole."

"Why do you call me an asshole?"

"For telling Livia about your senile escapade."

"It wasn't an escapade; it was a lot more than—"

"So much the worse."

"But Livia in the end was honest with me! She admitted having had an affair! I couldn't hide the fact that I, too—"

"Oh, give me a break! And above all, don't be such a hypocrite, you're not even good at it! The reason you told Livia you'd fucked the girl was not out of any sense of honesty, but out of spite. And you know what I say to you? That maybe what really drove you to sleep with that girl was Livia's silence, which made you jealous. So I confirm: You're an asshole."

"Look, Ingrid, my affair with Adriana—that was her name—was a rather complex matter. Among other things, everything that happened, happened because she wanted it to, for a specific purpose of her own."

"Did you go to Mass last Sunday?"

"What's that got to do with anything?"

"Because you're talking just like a Catholic! For true Catholics, it's always the woman who leads the man into temptation!"

"What, are we going to have a war of religion here? Let's drop it," said Montalbano, angry.

They sat a minute in silence, then Ingrid said in a low voice:

"I'm sorry."

"For what?"

"For what I said about the girl. It was stupid and vulgar."

"No, it wasn't, come on."

"Yes, it was. I saw that it hurt you to talk about it and so . . ."

"And so?"

"I had a jealous fit."

Montalbano felt at sea.

"Jealous? You're jealous of Livia?"

Ingrid laughed.

"No. Of Adriana."

"Adriana?!"

"Poor Salvo, you'll never understand women. So where do things stand now with Livia?"

"We don't know if it's worth the trouble to put the pieces back together or not."

"Look at me," said Ingrid.

Montalbano turned to look at her. She was very serious.

"It–is–worth–the–trouble. Let me tell you myself. Don't throw away all those years you've spent together. You think you don't have children but in fact you do. You have one: the past you've shared. I don't even have that."

Dazed, Montalbano saw two big tears fall from her eyes. He didn't know what to say. He wanted to embrace her, but he thought it would aggravate her moment of weakness. Ingrid stood up and went into the house.

When she returned, she had washed her face.

"Let's finish that bottle."

They did.

"Are you up to driving?"

"No," Ingrid replied in slurry voice. "You going to throw me out?"

"I wouldn't dream of it. Whenever you're ready, I'll drive you home."

"I wouldn't get in a car with you even if you were sober, so I'm certainly not going to get in with you now. Got any more whisky?"

"I should have another half bottle."

"Go get it."

They polished it off.

"I suddenly feel sleepy," said Ingrid.

She stood up, staggering a little, bent over, and kissed Montalbano on the forehead.

"Good night."

Montalbano went into the bathroom trying to make as little noise as possible, and when he got into bed, Ingrid, who had put on one of his shirts, was fast asleep.

7

He woke up later than usual, and with a bit of a headache.

Ingrid was still dead to the world. She hadn't moved all night from the position in which she had lain down. The scent of her skin ended up making Montalbano stay in bed a while longer, eyes closed and nostrils open. Then he got up gently and went to look out the window.

It wasn't raining, but it was hopeless. The sky was black and uniformly overcast.

He went into the bathroom, got dressed, made coffee, drank two cups, one after the other, then brought one to Ingrid.

"Good morning. I have to leave in a few minutes. If you want, you can stay in bed as long as you like."

"Wait for me. I'll take a quick shower and be ready in a jiffy. And I'd like another coffee, but I want to drink it with you."

He went into the kitchen to prepare another pot for four.

There was nothing in the house for breakfast, which he never ate. Sometimes there were little tubs of butter and jam in the refrigerator, but that was when Livia, who was in the habit of stealing them from hotels, would bring them with her during her stays at Marinella.

Montalbano set the small table in the kitchen as best he could, with a couple of small paper napkins, two demitasses, and a sugar bowl.

When Ingrid came in, the coffee had just finished bubbling up. They sat down and the inspector filled her cup.

For once, Montalbano felt a little awkward with her.

Maybe he shouldn't have opened up so much to Ingrid the previous evening; maybe he shouldn't have confided so much in her. She was Swedish, after all. Emotional reserve is a matter of religion for them. He probably made her feel embarrassed.

And if he had overstepped some boundary by telling her what had happened with Adriana, what right did he have to tell her of Livia's affair with Gianni? That was Livia's business and, at most, his, and it should have remained between them. On the other hand, with whom else besides Ingrid could he have talked about the situation?

You know why you happened to spill the beans with Ingrid? Because you're old and you can't handle mixing wine and whisky anymore, said Montalbano One.

Wine, whisky, and old age have nothing to do with it, Montalbano Two butted in. *How can you avoid bleeding from an open wound?*

Ingrid, however, didn't bring the previous evening's subject back up. It was clear she sensed Montalbano's uneasiness.

"What are you working on these days?"

"The local TV stations haven't been talking about anything else these last few days."

"I never watch the local TV stations. Or the national ones, for that matter."

"A dead girl was found in an illegal dump, murdered. We're having a very hard time identifying her. She was naked, without clothes or documents. Just a small tattoo."

"What kind of tattoo?"

"A moth."

"Where?" asked Ingrid, suddenly attentive.

"Right near her left shoulder blade."

"Oh my God!" said Ingrid, turning pale.

"What is it?"

"Until about three months ago I had a Russian house-keeper who had a tattoo just like that . . . How old was the girl who was killed?"

"Twenty-five, at the most."

"It fits. My girl was twenty-four. Oh my God!"

"Not so fast. It might not be her. Listen, why didn't you keep her as your housekeeper?"

"She suddenly disappeared!"

"What do you mean?"

"One morning I noticed she wasn't about the house. I asked the cook, but she hadn't seen her, either. So I went into her room, but she wasn't there. She never came back. I ended up replacing her with a woman from Zambia."

Right, as if she would ever replace her with someone from Bologna or Messina. Every time the inspector called Ingrid's house, the phone was answered by someone from Tananarive, Palikir, or Lilongwe . . .

"But her disappearance seemed suspicious to me," Ingrid continued.

"Why?"

"As you know, I'm hardly ever at home, but the few times I spoke to her—"

"How long did she stay with you?" Montalbano interrupted.

"A month and a few days. As I was saying, the few times I spoke with her she didn't make a good impression on me."

"Why not?"

"She was evasive, vague. She didn't want to tell me anything about herself."

"And after you became suspicious, what did you do?"

"I went to check the places where I kept my jewelry."

"You don't have a safe?"

"No. I keep them hidden in three different places. I never wear them, but once I did put some on, because I had to accompany my husband to an important dinner, and on that occasion, the girl must have figured out where I kept them."

"Did she steal them?"

"The ones in that particular hiding place, yes."

"Were they insured?"

"You must be kidding!"

"How much were they worth?"

"About three, four hundred thousand euros."

"Why didn't you report her?"

"My husband did report her!"

"To Montelusa Central?"

"No, the carabinieri."

So that was why he hadn't heard anything about it. Imagine the carabinieri ever keeping them informed about anything! But didn't the police, for their part, do the same with the carabinieri?

"What was her name?"

"She said it was Irina."

"But weren't you ever able to see any sort of identification papers?"

"No. Why should I?"

"Listen, how can you hire housekeepers, cooks, butlers . . . Your house is a revolving door."

"I'm not the one who hires them. The *ragioniere* Curcuraci does."

"And who's he?"

"He's the accountant who used to manage my father-in-law's estate, which is now my husband's."

"Have you got his phone number?"

"Yes, but it's on my cell phone, which I left in the car. When we go out now, I'll get it for you. Listen, if you want, I could . . . though I don't really like the idea at all . . ."

"You want to see the body?"

"If it would help you to identify her . . ."

"The shot that killed her practically took away her whole face. You wouldn't be able to recognize her. Unless . . . Listen, this Irina, did she have any distinguishing features you may have noticed?"

"In what sense?"

"Moles, scars . . ."

"On her face and hands, no. On other parts of her body, I couldn't say. It's not like I saw her naked or anything."

It was a stupid question.

"Wait," Ingrid continued . . . Would contact lenses be a distinguishing feature?"

"Why do you ask?"

"Because Irina wore them. One day, I remember, she lost one, but then we found it."

"Could you come with me to my office for five minutes? I want to show you a photograph."

"This is the second time," said Ingrid, standing up.

"For what?"

"The second time we're talking about an unknown person you're investigating and who I—"

"Right . . ." Montalbano said hesitantly.

Ingrid was referring to the time she saw on his desk the photograph of a drowned man who had been her lover, a fact that had enabled the inspector to break up a child-trafficking ring.

But Montalbano wasn't fond of remembering that case.

It had cost him an injury to his shoulder and, what weighed far more heavily on him, he had even been forced to kill a man.

"I have no doubts. The tattoo is the same," said Ingrid, handing the photograph back to the inspector, who set it down on the desk.

"Are you sure?"

"Absolutely certain."

Ingrid he could trust.

"Well, that's all. Thanks."

Ingrid gave him a big hug, which Montalbano returned. That moment of unease, when they were drinking their coffee in the kitchen, had entirely passed.

Naturally, that was the moment when the door opened and Mimì Augello appeared.

"Is this a bad moment?" he asked in a tone that made one want to pummel him.

"Not at all," said Ingrid. "I was just leaving."

"I'll show you out," said Montalbano.

"No need to bother," said Ingrid, stopping him with a light kiss on the lips. "And I mean it: Keep me informed."

She waved good-bye to Augello and went out.

"Ingrid's never liked me much," said Mimì.

"Did you ever give her a try?"

"Yes, but . . ."

"Sorry, but not all woman are yearning to be held in your manly arms."

"What's the matter this morning? A touch of bile? Nerves on edge? Something didn't go quite right last night?"

"Mimì, cut the shit, it's out of place. Ingrid came this

morning because she saw the photo of the tattoo on the Free Channel."

"Has Ingrid got the same tattoo? Did you check?"

"Mimì, has it ever dawned on you just how annoying these idiotic insinuations of yours are? If you don't feel like talking seriously, just go away and send in Fazio."

As if summoned, Fazio appeared.

"Come in, both of you, and sit down," said the inspector. "First of all, I want to know how things turned out with Signora Ciccina Picarella. Did she come yesterday evening?"

"Yes, she came rúnning," said Augello. "I had covered my rear by telling Gallo and Galluzzo to hang around and intervene as soon as the lady started yelling. Instead—"

"How did she react?"

"She took one look at the photograph and started laughing."

"What was so funny?"

"She was laughing, she explained, because the man in the photograph was most certainly not her husband, but someone who looked a great deal like him. A double. There was no way to convince her otherwise. And do you know, Salvo, why she acted that way?"

"Enlighten me, Master."

"She is so jealous, she is denying reality."

"But, Master, how do you manage to plumb such unfathomable depths of the human psyche? Do you use oxygen tanks or just hold your breath?"

"Salvo, when you put your mind to it, you're very good at acting like an asshole."

"But who says it's actually reality?" asked Fazio, doubtful.

"Are you in league with Signora Ciccina?" Augello reacted.

"Inspector, it's not a matter of being in league with her or not. Once I happened to run into my cousin Antonio on a street in Palermo. I stopped him, embraced him, and kissed him, and he kept looking at me like I was crazy. You see, he wasn't Antonio, but a spittin' image of him."

"So, how did you leave it with Signora Ciccina?" asked Montalbano.

"She said that she's going to see the commissioner this morning. She claims we concocted this whole business of the photograph just so we wouldn't have to keep looking for him."

"Mimì, you know what I say to you? This very morning, you put that photo in your pocket and go talk to the commissioner. Bonetti-Alderighi is liable to let Signora Ciccina persuade him and bring the roof down on our heads."

"I agree."

"Fazio, did you have time to do those searches?"

"Yessir. Between Montelusa, Vigàta, and nearby towns, there are four furniture works. As for cabinetmakers and restorers, there are two in Vigàta, four in Montelusa, and one in Gallotta. I've got the names and addresses, took them right out of the phone book."

"You probably ought to start checking them out."

"All right."

"Now, I'm going to make three phone calls, which I want the two of you to hear. We'll talk afterwards," said Montalbano.

He turned on the speakerphone.

"Cat? I would like you to ring up the *ragioniere* Curcuraci, at the following number—"

"Whawazzat, Chief? Culucaci?"

"Curcuraci."

"Culculupaci?"

"Never mind. I'll call him on the direct line."

"Hello, Ragioniere Curcuraci? Inspector Montalbano of Vigàta police here."

"Hello, Inspector. What can I do for you?"

"Ragioniere, I got your number from Signora Ingrid Sjostrom."

"I'm at your service."

"The lady told me you administer her husband's holdings and that, among your various responsibilities, you handle the hiring of housekeeping personnel . . ."

"That's correct."

"Since they're usually foreigners—"

"But always perfectly legitimate, Inspector!"

"I don't doubt that for a minute. What I want to know is, to whom do you turn for referrals?"

"Have you ever met Monsignor Pisicchio, by any chance?"

"I haven't had the pleasure."

"Monsignor Pisicchio is the head of a diocesan organiza-tion whose purpose is to help find arrangements for these poor unfortunate people who—"

"I get it, Ragioniere. So you would be in possession of information concerning a certain Irina—"

"Ah, her! What a wretch! Who bites the helping hand you hold out for her! Poor Monsignor Pisicchio was so upset about her! Anyway, I put all the information you want in my report to the carabinieri!"

"Have you got it within reach?"

"Just one minute, please."

Montalbano gestured to Fazio to write things down.

"Here we are, Irina Ilych, born at Schelkovo on May 15, 1983, passport number—"

"That'll be enough right there. Thank you, Ragioniere. If I need you for anything else, I'll give a call."

"Dr. Pasquano? Montalbano here."

"What can I do for you, dear friend?"

The inspector balked. How could this be? What was happening? No obscenities, no insults, no curses?

"Doctor, are you feeling all right?"

"I feel excellent, my friend. Why do you ask?"

"No, nothing. I wanted to ask you something about the girl with the tattoo."

"Go right ahead."

Montalbano was so flummoxed by Pasquano's politeness that he had trouble speaking.

"Did . . . did she wear contact lenses?"

"No."

"Couldn't they have fallen out when she was shot in the face?"

"No. That girl had never worn contact lenses. Of that I can assure you."

A light came on in Montalbano's mind.

"How did it go at the club last night, Doctor?"

Pasquano's laughter thundered in the room.

"You know what? I got the full house you wished me!"

"Really? So how did things turn out?"

"I stuck it to all of them! Just think, one of them raised me by . . ."

Montalbano hung up.

"Signor Graceffa? Montalbano here."

"Inspector, did you know I was just about to call you myself?"

"What did you want to tell me?"

"That I remembered the name of the town that Katya came from. I believe it was called Schickovo, or something like that."

"Could it have been Schelkovo?"

"Yes, that's it!"

"Signor Graceffa, I called you for another reason."

"I'm happy to help."

"After Katya left, did you happen to check and see if she took anything from your home?"

"What would she have taken?"

"I dunno, silverware, something that used to belong to your wife . . ."

"Inspector, Katya was an honest girl!"

"Okay, but have you checked?"

"No, I haven't, but . . ."

"Go on."

"Iss a delicate matter."

"You know I'm silent as the tomb."

"Are you alone in your office? Is there anyone there who can hear me?"

"I'm completely alone; you can speak freely."

"Well . . . in short . . . that night I told you 'bout . . . when I went to see Katya to . . . you remember?"

"Perfectly."

"Okay . . . I told the girl I would give her my wife's earrings if she . . . I even showed them to her . . . they're really

beautiful ... but she wouldn't budge ... 'no' meant 'no' ...
You know what I mean?

"Absolutely."

The old-fashioned gentleman was ready to give the girl
the earrings, a memento of his dead wife, if she would sleep
with him.

"Have you had a chance since then to check if those
earrings—"

"Well ... just day before yesterday, those earrings, along
with a necklace and two bracelets, well, I gave them to my
niece Concetta, and so—"

"Thank you, Signor Graceffa."

"So, would you please explain to us what's going on?" asked
Mimì.

"The situation is as follows: Signor Graceffa had a home
care assistant by the name of Katya who came from Schelkovo
and had a tattoo of a moth very near to her left shoulder blade.
Incidentally, by now I no longer have any reason to doubt
Signor Graceffa's eyesight. My friend Ingrid Sjostrom, as confirmed by Ragioniere Curcuraci, had a housekeeper named
Irina who came from Schelkovo and had the exact same tattoo.
Except that Irina was a thief and Katya wasn't. Irina, however,
wore contact lenses and Katya had black hair. The murdered
girl therefore can't be either Katya or Irina, but she does have
the exact same tattoo as the other two. What do you think?"

"That three identical tattoos all in the same place can't be
a coincidence," said Augello.

8

"I agree with you," said Montalbano. "It can't be a simple coincidence. It might be a sign of membership, a kind of emblem."

"Membership in what?"

"How should I know, Mimì? A society of cuckoo-clock lovers, a club of Russian salad eaters, or some cult that worships a female rock star . . . Don't forget that these are very young women, and that tattoo may well date back to when they were in high school or whatever it is they have in Schelkovo."

"But why a moth of all things?" asked Augello.

"Dunno. Maybe a tattoo of an elephant or a rhinoceros would look out of place on a pretty girl."

Silence descended.

"What are we going to do?" Mimì asked a few moments later.

"For now, I want to check something," said Montalbano.

"Can I begin to make the rounds of the furniture makers and restorers?" Fazio asked in turn.

"Yes. The sooner you start, the better."

"What about me?" asked Augello.

"I've already told you: Put the photo of Picarella in your pocket and run to see the commissioner. Do as I say. We'll meet back up at five this afternoon. Oh, and please send in Catarella."

As the two were leaving, Montalbano wrote something on a half sheet of paper. Catarella shot in like a ball on a tether.

"Your orders, Chief!"

"On this piece of paper you'll find two names: Graceffa and Monsignor Pisicchio. I even wrote down Graceffa's number for you. I want you to call him up and ask him for the surname of his sister, whose first name is Carmela, as well as her telephone number and address. Afterwards, I want you to find Monsignor Pisicchio's number in the phone book, call him up, and then put him through to me. Is that clear?"

"Chryssal clear, Chief."

Five minutes later the phone rang.

"Pisicchio."

"Ah, Monsignor. Chief Inspector Montalbano of Vigàta here. Excuse me if I took the liberty of—"

"Why do you want to know my sister's married name and telephone number?" the other interrupted.

It was clear from his tone that the monsignor was a tad pissed off. *Matre santa*, what had Catarella done?

"No, Monsignor, I'm very sorry, the switchboard operator must have . . . you see, your sister isn't . . . Forgive me, I wanted to come and talk to you this morning about an investigation—"

"Does it involve my sister?"

"In no way whatsoever, Monsignor."

"Then come at twelve o'clock sharp. Via del Vescovado 48. And please be punctual."

The communication terminated without good-byes. A man of few words, this Monsignor Pisicchio.

"Catarella!"

"Here I am, Chief! I got Gracezza's sister's number!"

"But why did you ask for the name and number of the monsignor's sister as well?"

Catarella balked.

"But din't you want the nummers of both sisters, Gracezza's and Monsignor Pisicchio's?"

"Forget about it, just give me the number Graceffa gave you and make yourself scarce."

Catarella went out feeling humiliated and offended. Naturally, in the number he wrote down, one couldn't tell the threes from the eights and the fives from the sixes. The inspector was lucky enough to get it right the first time.

"Mrs. Loporto?"

"Yes? Who's this?"

"Inspector Montalbano here. I got your telephone number from your brother Beniamino. I need to talk to you."

"To me?"

"Yes, signora."

"And why should I speak to you? What is this anyway? My conscience is clean!"

"I have no doubt of that. I simply need a little information from you."

"Ha ha ha! Now I get it!"

Signora Loporto cackled sardonically.

"What do you get?"

"There's no more tripe for the cats, my friend!"

"I don't understand, signora."

"But I understand *you* perfectly! Like the other time you came here asking for information and you sold me a vacuum cleaner that didn't work!"

Perhaps it was better to change tone.

"All right, then, in five minutes two police officers are going to come pick you up and bring you into the station."

"So you really are a cop?"

"Yes. And I advise you to answer my question: When you were looking for a home care assistant to look after your brother, who did you turn to?"

"To Patre Pinna."

"And who's he?"

"Whattya mean, 'who's he'? He's a priest. The priest of my parish!"

"And was he the one who put you in touch with the Russian girl, Katya?"

"No. Patre Pinna told me to talk to Monsignor Pisicchio, who's in Montelusa."

"And was it Monsignor Pisicchio who sent you Katya?"

"It was someone working for the monsignor."

Tangled like the intestines in one's belly, the streets of old Montelusa, with their "No Entry" signs, the never-ending roadworks, the overflowing garbage bins, the rubble of a townhouse that had collapsed two months earlier still blocking half of a narrow street, saw to it that the inspector arrived at ten minutes past twelve.

"You're late," said Monsignor Pisicchio, looking at him with scorn. "And to think I even told you to be sure to be punctual!"

"I'm very sorry, but the traffic—"

"And do you think the traffic is some sort of novelty? In other words, if one knows there's always traffic, then one leaves home earlier and doesn't arrive late."

Monsignor Pisicchio was a big, burly man of about fifty with red hair and the build and manner of an ex-rugbyman. All the furnishings in his office in the bishopric were proportionate to the monsignor's bulk, including the crucifix behind the desk, which, like the monsignor, cast a harsh eye on the inspector, or so it seemed, at least to Montalbano, for having arrived late.

"I'm truly mortified," he said, fearing some sort of corporal punishment.

"What do you want from me?"

"I'm told that you're the head of an organization involved in finding work for—"

"Yes, the 'organization,' as you call it, is an association created five years ago and it has a name: It's called 'Benevolence.' Our activities are strictly confined to very young girls, to keep them from falling into shady or underworld circuits like drugs or prostitution ..."

"How many are you?"

"Six, apart from me. Three men and three women. All volunteers blessed, naturally, with benevolence."

"How do the girls manage to find you?"

"In many ways. Some just show up on their own, alone, having learned in one way or another of our existence. Others are pointed out to us by parish priests or associations like ours, others by ordinary people. And others still we are able to persuade to give up whatever they were doing and put their trust in us."

"How do you persuade them?" asked the inspector, hoping that the means of persuasion didn't include strong-arm tactics in keeping with the rugbyman's character.

"Our volunteers approach them on the streets where they've started prostituting themselves, or in certain nightspots ... To make a long story short, we try to get to them in time, before the irreparable happens."

"How many of them accept your help?"

"More than you can possibly imagine. A lot of girls are aware of the dangers and prefer an honest job to easy money."

"Do any girls ever get tired of the honest jobs and go back to the easy money?"

"Rarely."

"Could I speak to your volunteers?"

"That's not a problem."

He searched about on his desk, picked up a sheet of paper, and handed it to the inspector.

"Here are their names, addresses, and telephone numbers."

"Thank you. I'm here about two Russian girls, Katya and Irina, which your organization—I'm sorry, your association, had—"

"I've been told, unfortunately, about this Irina. But I'm not the person to talk to about her."

"Who is, then?"

"You see, I legally and officially represent Benevolence, I preside over it, find the funding for it, but would you believe that, in these five years, I have never seen even one of these girls?"

"So to whom should I address myself?"

"To the first name on that list. Cavaliere Guglielmo Piro; he is, so to speak, our operative arm."

"Does your organization—sorry, association—have a headquarters?"

"Yes. Two small rooms in Via Empedocle 12. You'll find all the information on the sheet I gave you."

"What are their hours?"

"At Via Empedocle there's only someone there after seven in the evening. During the day my volunteers are working, you see. Anyway, to do what we do, the telephone is quite sufficient. But that's enough questions for now. You'll have to excuse me, but I have an engagement. If you had been good enough to get here on time . . ."

Since he was already in Montelusa, he dropped in at the studios of the Free Channel.

Nicolò Zito told him at once that he didn't have much time and was about to go on the air with the one o'clock report.

"You know, about those photos: Except for the two phone calls the first day, we haven't received any others."

"Does that seem odd to you?"

"A little. Should I keep showing them on the air?"

"Do it again today, and then you can stop."

Montalbano, too, was surprised at the scarcity of testimonies. Normally, using television in the search for a missing person triggered a deluge of phone calls from people who had actually seen the person, people who thought they had seen the person, and people who hadn't seen anything at all but decided to call anyway. This time, however, there had only been two calls, and both, moreover, had been completely useless.

It was raining lightly when he pulled up in front of the trattoria. As there still was no fresh fish, as a first course Enzo brought him a dish of pasta with *pesto alla trapanese*, and as a second, *piscistoccu alla ghiotta*, stockfish prepared according to the Messinese recipe.

All things considered, Montalbano felt he had little to complain about, even if he wasn't particularly fond of stockfish.

When he left the trattoria it was still raining lightly, so he went to headquarters.

According to the sheet that Monsignor Pisicchio had given him, Cavaliere Guglielmo Piro, first on the list as the operative arm, had three telephone numbers—an office, home, and cell number. Quite likely at that hour the cavaliere was at home, resting after his midday meal. Using his direct line, the inspector called the first number.

"Hello? Is this the Piro home? Yes? Chief Inspector Montalbano here. Is Cavaliere Piro there?"

"You wait, I get him," said a girl's voice.

Apparently the cavaliere made use of his association in his own home.

"Hello? I didn't understand who this is."

"Cavaliere, I'm Inspector Montalbano. I urgently need to see you."

"About a house?"

What was he talking about? What did houses have to do with this?

"No, I need some information from you about a few Russian girls who—"

"I understand. Since my main occupation is selling houses, I thought . . . Who gave you my number?"

"Monsignor Pisicchio, who also gave me a flyer of your association, Benevolence."

There. He'd managed not to call it an organization.

"Ah. So we could meet later at Via Empedocle."

"Okay. Tell me what time."

"Six o'clock okay with you? If you'd like to see me sooner, you could come to my real estate office, which is in Via—"

"No, thank you, Cavaliere, six o'clock is perfectly fine with me."

He had a moment of doubt. What if everyone at Benevolence was as obsessive as Monsignor Pisicchio?

"I should warn you that I may arrive a little late."

"No problem. I'll wait for you."

The first to report back at five was Mimì Augello.

"Did you see the commissioner?"

"Did you know that Signora Ciccina had already spoken to him?"

"Well, what a surprise! The lady was probably at the commissioner's at the crack of dawn! In short, what did he say to you?"

"That we've been taking the kidnapping too lightly. That we immediately drew the conclusion that it was all staged, and so we didn't conduct any serious searches. That we've been too slapdash. That he's not the least bit inclined to defend us if it turns out that a kidnapping indeed occurred. That we have no authorization whatsoever to think that Signora Ciccina might not be right. That the man in the photo may well be a double. That the popular belief that every person has six identical copies in the world may not be so far-fetched. That—"

"That's enough. To conclude?"

"Remember Pontius Pilate?"

Fazio came in.

"You got anything big for me?"

"No, Chief, I'm empty-handed. And anyway, I'm moving too slowly."

"Why do you say that?"

"Because I don't know what I'm supposed to ask, I don't

know what I'm supposed to do, I don't know where I'm supposed to look. At any rate, I began with the two restorers and the one furniture works here in town."

"Tell me about 'em."

"The Januzzi furniture works went out of business a year ago. The store is open for a clearance sale of the pieces they've still got remaining, but the big warehouse where they used to make them is shut down, and nobody works there anymore. I looked at the padlocks on the doors, and they're all rusted. I can guarantee you they haven't been touched for months."

"And what about the restorers?"

"One of them works in a shop about fifteen feet by fifteen, and he's only a restorer in a manner of speaking. He repairs wicker chairs, dressers missing a leg, that sort of thing. He keeps the stuff he needs to work on out on the sidewalk, then piles it all up inside in the evening. The other guy is a real restorer. I talked to him, and his name is Filippo Todaro. He had a little purpurin and showed it to me. He explained that he only needs a little bit to restore the gilded pieces. Just a few grams."

"Are you telling me we should forget about restorers?"

"That's right, Chief."

"Okay. I remember you said that there were only four furniture makers that need to be checked out."

"Yes, but . . ."

"You think there's no point in it?"

"Yessir. *Nuttata persa e figlia femmina.*"

"Don't get discouraged, Fazio. By tomorrow, you'll be done. Believe me, it's too important. You've got to check them out."

"I can take two," said Mimì, moved to pity by Fazio's disconsolate face.

"But why do you think it's pointless?" Montalbano insisted.

"I can't put it into words, Chief. It's a feeling."

"You want to know something?" said the inspector. "I have the same feeling as you. So let's finish our check of the furniture makers and afterwards, when we've come to the conclusion that we're on the wrong track, we'll start looking for another."

"Whatever you say, Chief."

Since another downpour had broken out and the windshield wipers were having trouble removing the water from the glass, the inspector went crazy trying to find fucking Via Empedocle. When, at last, he turned onto it, he noticed there wasn't room to park so much as a needle. He managed to park on a nearly parallel little street called Via Platone. Given that he was in a philosophical neighborhood, he decided to take the whole situation philosophically.

He waited inside his car for the rain to let up, then got out, made a quick dash, and arrived at the apartment a quarter of an hour late. But there were no recriminations.

"I would like, first of all, to know what your work entails."

"The work we do is actually quite simple," said Cavaliere Guglielmo Piro.

He was a well-dressed, rather midgetlike man of about sixty, with not a single hair on his head to save his life, and he had a tic: Every three minutes or so he would rapidly slide the index finger of his right hand under his nose. The first of the two small rooms was a kind of reception area with chairs, armchairs, and a sofa; the second room, the one the inspector and the cavaliere were in, had a computer, three file cabinets, two telephones, and two desks.

"The point is to figure out which of the available girls has the necessary requisites to satisfy the particular needs of the people who come to us. Once we've found the right girl, we put her in touch with the applicant. And there you have it."

There you have it, my ass, thought Montalbano, who had taken an immediate dislike to the cavaliere for no plausible reason.

"And what are the particular needs of your clients?"

The cavaliere slid his finger under his nose three times.

"I'm sorry, Inspector, but 'clients' is not the right word."

"Then what is the right word?"

"I wouldn't know. But I would like it to be clear that the people who come to us looking for a girl don't pay a cent. Ours is a social service, not-for-profit, the purpose of which is to rescue and—why not?—to redeem—"

"Okay, but where does the money come from?"

Cavaliere Piro's face looked troubled by the brutality of the question.

"Providence."

"And who's hidden behind that pseudonym?"

This time the cavaliere became irritated.

"We've got nothing to hide, you know. We get help from a lot of people, including donations, and then there are the regional and provincial administrations, not to mention town hall, the bishopric, charitable contributions . . ."

"Not the national government?"

"Yes, in a small way."

"How much?"

"Eighty euros a day for each guest."

Which was a pretty fair contribution, however "small," as the cavaliere called it.

"How many girls have you got at the moment?"

"Twelve. But we're at our limit."

Which came to 960 euros a day. Calculating an average of ten girls a year, that meant 292,000 euros. And that was the least of it? Not bad for a not-for-profit association.

Montalbano was beginning to smell a rat.

9

There was, moreover, something in the cavaliere's attitude that seemed fishy to the inspector. Was he resentful of the way the inspector was asking him questions, or was he afraid he might ask the right question? One that the cavaliere might have trouble answering? And, if so, what was the right question?

"Have you got a place for the girls to stay while they are awaiting placement?" Montalbano asked, taking a wild stab.

"Of course. There's a little villa a bit outside of Montelusa."

"Do you own it?"

"I wish! No, we pay a rather high rent for it."

"To whom?"

"To a company based in Montelusa. It's called Mirabilis."

"Have you got a staff assigned to it?"

"Yes, a permanent staff. But we also need outside people, temporary workers."

"Such as?"

"Well, doctors, to give one example."

"In case the girls get sick?"

"Not only in case of illness. You see, every new girl who comes here is immediately given a medical examination."

"To see if she has any sexually transmitted diseases?"

Cavaliere Piro did not hide his annoyance at the question. He furrowed his brow, raised his eyes to the heavens, and ran his finger under his nose, all to fine comic effect.

"That, too, naturally. But mostly to find out if they have healthy and strong constitutions. You know, with the wretched lives they were forced to lead before . . ."

"Are the doctors paid by you?"

"No, we have an arrangement with the bishopric, and so—"

Imagine them ever coughing up a lira!

"Do you get the medications free as well?"

"Naturally."

Naturally. How could you go wrong?

"Let's backtrack a moment. I asked you what the particular needs that you alluded to were."

"Well, there are people who want home care, others who want a housekeeper, others a cook. Understand?"

"Perfectly. Is that all?"

The cavaliere rubbed his nose.

"Age and religion are also important."

"Anything else?"

Nose rubbed at the threshold of the speed of sound.

"What else could they want?"

"I don't know . . . hair color . . . eye color . . . length of legs . . . breast measurement . . . waist measurement . . ."

"Why would they make such requests?"

"You know, Cavaliere, there might be some old geezer dreaming of a home care assistant who looks like the blue fairy."

The cavaliere ran first his right forefinger, then his left, under his nose. Montalbano changed the subject.

"What's the average age?"

"At a rough guess, I'd say twenty-seven, twenty-eight."

"But these girls come to you from an entirely different universe. How do they learn to become cooks or housekeepers?"

Guglielmo Piro looked a little relieved.

"It doesn't take them long, you know. They're very sharp girls. And whenever we notice that one of them has a particular knack for something, we help her, so to speak, to perfect herself . . ."

"Let me get this straight. Do you hire instructors to teach them how to cook, how to—"

"What need is there to hire instructors? They learn from our own staff."

And that way they also saved on labor costs.

"Monsignor Pisicchio told me that some girls are brought to your attention by parish priests, others by associations like yours, and others still are directly recruited . . ."

The cavaliere ran his finger frantically under his nose.

"Good God, what an ugly word! 'Recruited'!"

"Have I said the wrong thing again? Please forgive me, Cavaliere, I have a rather limited vocabulary. How would you yourself describe it?"

"Bah, I dunno . . . persuaded . . . saved, that's it."

"And how are they persuaded to be saved?"

"Well, every now and then Masino takes it upon himself and makes the rounds on the nightclub circuit."

"That must be an onerous task."

Cavaliere Piro didn't grasp the irony.

"Yes," he said.

"Does he limit himself to Sicilian nightclubs?"

"Yes."

"Does he pay for his, er, entertainment out of his own pocket?"

"That would be nice! No, he presents us with a list of expenses."

"So how does he work?"

"Well, once he notices a girl a little, how shall I say, different from the others—"

"Different in what way?"

"More reserved ... less open to the sexual advances the clients make at her ... Then Masino approaches her and starts to talk to her. Masino is, how shall I say, rather loquacious."

"Loquacious! Thank you for enriching my vocabulary. Does Masino make these rounds every night?"

"Heavens, no! Only Saturday nights. Otherwise, staying up all hours of the night, his work would go, how shall I say ..."

"To pot?"

The Cavaliere shot him a scornful glance.

"To the dogs."

"What's Masino's full name?"

"Tommaso Lapis, which would be the third name on the list that the monsignor gave you. But Anna also sometimes does the same thing. Anna Degregorio is the fourth name on the list."

"Anna Degregorio hangs out alone in nightclubs?"

"Absolutely not. She's a very attractive girl, and that could give rise to misunderstandings. She goes with her boyfriend, who does not, however, belong to our association."

"But he knows how to combine benefit and delight."

"I'm not sure what you—"

"Does the young lady also present a list of expenses?"

"Of course."

"And does she also go out on Saturday nights?"

"No, Sundays. She has Mondays off."

"What does she do for a living?"

"She's a hairdresser."

"Listen, I'll tell you now why I wanted to meet with you. I'm going to give you two names: Irina and Katya, Russian, both a little over twenty, both born in Schelkovo."

"I imagined that's what it was, you know. Has Irina got into trouble again? Ragioniere Curcuraci complained bitterly to us about the theft of Signora Sjostrom's jewelry. But there's no way we can guarantee the ethical conduct of these girls. So what's she done this time?"

"I don't know that she's gotten into any more trouble. I know that Irina's surname is Ilych. I would like to know Katya's surname."

"Wait just a minute."

He went over to the computer and fiddled around a bit.

"Katya Lissenko, born at Schelkovo on the third of April, 1984. Did she do something wrong, too?"

"I don't think so."

"It says here that we placed her as an assistant at the home of a Vigàta man, Beniamino Graceffa. Is she still working for him?"

"No, she left. Did she ever get back in touch with you?'

"No, we never heard from her again."

"And what about Irina?"

"Never heard from her, either, and anyway, if we had, we would have been forced to have her arrested. It couldn't be helped. We are absolutely respectful of—"

"Have you had many cases where the girls have disappointed you, betrayed your trust?"

"Only twice, fortunately. An almost laughable percentage, as you can see. Irina and a Nigerian girl."

"What did the Nigerian do?"

"She pulled a knife on the lady she was working for. It

happened about four years ago. We haven't had any other complaints, thank God."

The inspector couldn't think of any other questions to ask. He continued to smell a rat, even stronger than before, but had been unable to tell where the smell was coming from. He stood up.

"Thank you for everything, Cavaliere. If I need you again in the future—"

"I am entirely at your disposal. Let me show you out."

When he was in the doorway, Montalbano thought to ask:

"Do you remember if Katya and Irina arrived at the same time at your association?"

The cavaliere answered without hesitation.

"They came together, I remember it perfectly."

"How come?"

"They were very frightened. Terrified, in fact. Michelina—whose name is the second one on the list—is the person in charge of welcoming new arrivals—didn't know what to do. She had to call me to help her calm them down a little."

"Did they tell you why they were so frightened?"

"No. But it's not hard to figure out."

"Meaning?"

"They had probably escaped from their—how shall I say?—exploiters, without giving notice."

"What makes you think they were being exploited? They weren't prostitutes, as far as we know, but dancers."

"Of course. But maybe they hadn't finished paying who-ever it was who had them come to Italy. You know how these expatriations work, don't you? Their friend, on the other hand, arrived a week later."

Certainly a surprise blow to the head from a billy club would have had less of an effect on Montalbano.

"Th–their . . . f–friend?"

The cavaliere was bewildered by Montalbano's extreme bewilderment.

"Yes . . . Sonya Meyerev, also from Schelkovo. She—"

"Where did you place her?"

"We didn't have enough time to place her, because after a week with us, she didn't come home to the villa one evening. She disappeared."

"But didn't you ask her friends if they knew anything?"

"Of course we did. But Irina reassured us, saying that Sonya had run into a friend of her father's and that she—"

"Was it Masino who persuaded all three to come to your association?"

"No. They showed up of their own accord."

"Have you got photos of the girls?"

"I've got photocopies of their passports."

"Let's go back inside. I want them."

As the cavaliere was printing them off the computer, Montalbano asked him:

"Would you give me the address of the villa where the girls live?"

"Certainly. It's on the road to Montaperto. Just past the filling station. It's a rather large villa . . ."

"How large?"

"Three floors. You'll recognize it at once."

The little villa had suddenly grown considerably in size.

"Do the girls eat there?"

"Yes. We employ a cook and a maid. There's also a woman, a sort of manager, who sleeps there with them. Sometimes our guests get a little restless. They quarrel over the silliest things, get into fights, do things to spite one another."

"Can I go there?"

"Where?"

"To the little villa."

The cavaliere did not look pleased.

"Well, at this hour ... The night watchman is already on duty. He has explicit orders not to let anyone in. As you can imagine, with all those women there, some good-for-nothings might try to ... If you like, I could phone ahead and ... but I don't really see why you ..."

"Do the maid and the cook also sleep there?"

"The cook, yes. The maid, no. She comes in at nine in the morning and works until one P.M."

"Write down the first and last name of the maid, along with her address and telephone number."

It was the first thing he did as soon as he got home. He set the photocopies down on the table and phoned.

"Signora Ernestina Vullo? This is Inspector Montalbano."

"Inspector for what?"

"The police."

"Listen, I kicked my son 'Ntoniu right outta the house on 'is ass. Is he a legal adult?"

"Who?" asked Montalbano, a bit numb and wondering if the question was addressed to him.

"My son. Is he a legal adult?"

"I wouldn't know."

"Of course he's a legal adult! He's thirty years old! So you just go look for 'im wherever the hell he happens a be jerking off and don' come lookin' for him anymore at my house. Good-b—"

"Wait, signora, don't hang up! I'm not calling you about your son, but about your job with the Benevolence Association, where they lodge—"

"—those sluts! Those nasty little tarts! Hussies! Whores! Easy women! Forget about it, Inspector! Just imagine, in the morning the bitches walk all around the place naked!"

Exactly what he wanted to know.

"Listen, signora, please try to think calmly before answering. Try to remember as best you can. Some time ago there were three Russian girls at the villa: Irina, Sonya, and Katya. Do you remember them?"

"Sure. Katya was a good girl. Sonya ran away."

"Did you happen to notice if all three girls had the same tattoo near the left shoulder blade?"

"Yessir, a butterfly."

"All three of them?"

"All three of them. All the same exack butterfly."

"Did you notice when the television news showed—"

"I don't watch television."

Was it any use having her come down to the station to show her the photos?

He decided against it.

"One time, but iss been two years now," the woman continued, "I saw a tattoo on a Russian girl's left shoulder blade, in the same exack place where the others had a butterfly."

"Was it a different kind of butterfly?"

"No, sir, it wasn't no butterfly . . . Wait a second, I can't remember how iss called . . . iss called . . . ah, that's it: *cululùchira.*"

O matre santa, what could that be? A buttock tattoo? Wasn't that a bit excessive, even for a nightclub dancer?

"Could you explain to me what that is?"

"Don'tcha know what it is? Good god, everybody knows what that is! So how'm I gonna 'splain you what it is?"

"Try."

"Well . . . less say iss almos' big as a fly, it flies around at night, an' it makes light."

A firefly.

The moment he set down the receiver, the phone rang.

"Signor Montalbano? Adelina here."

"Hello, Adelì. What is it?"

"Did you forget, signore?"

"Forget what, Adelina?"

"That my boy wanneta see you."

He'd completely forgotten about it.

"You know, Adelì, I've been so busy that—"

"My boy says iss urgent."

"I'll go see him tomorrow morning, I promise. Good night, Adelì."

The moment he set down the receiver, the phone rang.

Since he had the phone in his hand, he used it.

"Fazio?"

"What is it, Chief?"

"Sorry to bother you at home."

"Come on, Chief!"

"Did you manage to find anything out at the furniture works?"

"Inspector Augello and I decided that I would go check out the two in Montelusa. Took me only an hour to do everything. The first one makes modern furniture, without any gilding. The second one used to gild occasionally, up until two years ago. I asked the owner if he kept any purpurin around, and he said that the little they had left they threw away."

"So are we on the wrong track, as you were saying?"

"I'd say so."

"Let's wait and see what Augello says, then we'll decide. So, will you have a little time tomorrow morning?"

"Of course. What do you want me to do?"

"I found out that the Russian girls we've been talking about were lodged in a villa rented by Benevolence, which is an association presided over by Monsignor Pisicchio, the purpose of which is to find work for these girls. The monsignor's right-hand man, Cavaliere Guglielmo Piro, who has a real estate agency, told me the villa belongs to a Montelusa company called Mirabilis. It's large, a three-story villa on the road to Montaperto, after the filling station."

"You want me to go there?"

"No. I want to know who's in this Mirabilis company, the names of the people on the board of directors, the other members ... I want to find out what's officially known, but, above all, what is being kept from becoming officially known."

"I'll try."

"I haven't finished, sorry."

"Go on."

"I also want to know everything about this Cavaliere Guglielmo Piro since the time he was born. As I said, he runs a real estate agency in Montelusa. I want to know what people say about him."

"He seems fishy to you?"

"What can I say? This whole association seems fishy to me. It's just an intuition, though. Maybe the Monsignor doesn't even know, but it's possible that, behind his back ..."

"I'll get going on it early tomorrow morning."

It wasn't raining, though the weather remained bad. The sea had withdrawn from the edge of the veranda, retreating halfway down the beach. He could eat outside.

He savored a bowl of caponata, accompanying it with bread made of durum wheat, a bread he liked so much that sometimes, when it was fresh, he would break it with his hands and wolf it down by itself, pure and simple.

Before starting to ring, the phone politely waited until he had finished eating.

10

"Salvo, it's me."

Livia!

He had stopped waiting for her call. After what they had said to each other the last time, he didn't think she would call him back. If anything, it was he who should have called back. And he had tried to do so, but had found nobody home and thus given up. Without persisting, and feeling even a bit relieved at having avoided the discussion. Because to continue to talk to each other by phone would have been pointless; it might even make things worse. They had to meet in person and talk. And this was precisely what frightened him. The tiniest thing, the wrong word, a minor angry outburst, might send them both down a path of no return. Meanwhile they were both left hanging as though in mid-air, like children's balloons which, half-emptied of helium, can't manage either to rise to the sky or fall to the ground.

With each passing day, this sort of limbo became worse than a living hell.

Immediately the sound of her voice made his heart jump. He felt his mouth go dry and had trouble speaking.

"I'm so happy to hear from you. Really."

"What were you doing?"

"I've just finished eating dinner on the veranda. Luckily it stopped raining, because it's been days—"

"Here it's not raining. Were you able to sit outside in shirtsleeves?"

"Yes, it wasn't cold."

"What did you eat?"

Then he understood. Livia was trying to be there with him, at his house in Marinella. She was imagining him the way she had seen him so many times before, trying to annul the distance by picturing him as he performed the customary acts he did every evening. He was suddenly overwhelmed by a feeling that was a mixture of melancholy, tenderness, regret, and desire.

"Caponata," he said in a choked-up voice.

How on earth was it possible to get a lump in one's throat simply by uttering the word "caponata"?

"Why did you stop calling?"

"I tried a few nights ago, but you didn't answer. After that I didn't—"

"You didn't feel like trying anymore?"

He was about to answer that he hadn't had the time, but he refrained, preferring to tell the truth.

"I didn't have the courage."

"Me neither."

"How come you decided to call tonight?"

"Because we can't go on this way."

"That's true."

Silence descended.

But Montalbano continued to hear Livia's slightly panting breath. Was it only because she was talking to him that she was breathing like that? Was it emotion, or was it something else?

"How are you?" he asked her.

"How do you think? What about you?"

"I'm certainly not feeling very good."

"But are you working?"

"Yes, I've got a case on my hands that—"

"You're lucky."

"Why?"

"Because you can distract yourself. I, on the other hand, couldn't take it anymore."

"What do you mean?"

"I called in sick. It's not a complete lie; I have a little fever every day."

"Every day? Have you called the doctor?"

"Yes, it's nothing serious. I have to take a boring series of tests. At any rate, starting yesterday, I can stay home for two weeks. I couldn't take going to the office any longer. You know what I mean?" She laughed cheerlessly. "For the first time, I made a big mess at work and was reprimanded."

Then, without thinking, since it came from the bottom of his heart, he said:

"But if you're not going to the office, why don't you come down here?"

A few moments passed before Livia resumed speaking.

"Is that really what you want?"

"Get on a flight tomorrow. I'll come get you at the airport. Come on, there's no need to think it over."

"Isn't it better to wait?"

"Wait for what?"

"For you to solve the case you're working on. I don't think you'd have much time for me if I came tomorrow."

"I'll drop everything."

"Salvo, you know that in the end you wouldn't be able to. You would start finding excuses that I don't think I could stand to hear, the way things are now."

"I promise I'll—"

"I know all about your promises."

Montalbano thought: *Here are the wrong words I was afraid of. Now the usual squabbling will begin.* Instead, Livia added:

"Anyway, I don't think we would be able to talk about us if we just saw each other on the run. We have to be able to look one another in the eye as we speak, for however long it takes."

She was right.

"So, what'll we do?"

"Let's do this. As soon as you know you're going to have a few days off, really off, call me up, and I'll come. Okay?"

"Okay."

"We'll talk again soon."

"Okay."

"Have a good sleep."

"You too."

"I . . . I'll be in touch."

And they hung up. Montalbano had the distinct impression that Livia was about to say *I love you*, but her embarrassment had prevented her. He felt so moved that he could hardly breathe. He ran out on the veranda, grabbed the railing with his hand, and took a deep breath. Then he sat down and laid his head on his folded arms.

There was a note of sadness in Livia's voice so profound that it was making him feel ill. Only one other time had he heard the same note in Livia's words: when she had spoken about the child she could no longer have.

He slept poorly, the usual tossing and turning, the usual getting up and going back to bed, the usual flicking the light on and off to look at the hands of the clock, which seemed to be moving in slow motion.

At last he saw the glow of a clear dawn filter in through the window.

He got up feeling hopeful. Maybe the fisherman had been wrong about how long the bad weather would last. And that was indeed the case. The sky was pure, the air cool and crisp. The sea wasn't calm yet, but neither was it so rough as to prevent the fishing boats from going out. He felt comforted by the thought that he could finally eat fresh fish at Enzo's.

So comforted that he went back to bed and slept for three hours straight to make up for the sleep he'd lost.

Leaving the house, he decided not to drop in at the station but to go immediately to the prison a few miles outside Montelusa. He had no authorization whatsoever to speak with the inmate, but he was counting on his good friendship with the warden, a woman who understood things.

And, in fact, it took him no time at all to find himself in a small room face-to-face with Pasquale, Adelina's son.

"When are they going to grant you house arrest?"

"Just a few more days. Supposedly the judge needs to think it over. What's there to think about? The horns on his head? But I couldn't wait any longer to tell you what I have to tell you."

"And what do you have to tell me?"

"Inspector, this is very important. I mean it. Even though I'm in here with you, I never said anything to you. Know what I mean?"

"Exactly."

"So that's the deal: You never met with Pasquale Cirrinciò in prison. I don't wanna get a reputation for being a rat."

"I give you my word."

"Have you identified the dead girl you found at the dump?"

"Not yet, unfortunately."

Pasquale stopped to think this over a moment, then said:

"The other evening when I was watching TV, they showed two photographs."

Montalbano pricked up his ears. He had been ready for anything, except for Pasquale to tell him something connected to his ongoing investigation.

"You mean the butterfly tattoo?"

"Yessir."

"You'd seen it before?"

"Yessir."

"On a girl's body?"

"No, sir, in a photograph."

"Go on. Don't make me have to pry the words out of you."

"Do you remember Peppi Cannizzaro?"

"No. Who is he?"

"He was charged with armed robbery at the Banca Regionale of Montelusa. They kept him inside for a few months, then let 'im go 'cause they din't have no proof."

"But did he do it?"

Pasquale brought his face so close to the inspector's that it looked like he wanted to kiss him.

"Yes, but they din't have no proof."

"Okay, and what's Peppi Cannizzaro got to do with—"

"Lemme explain. They took Peppi Cannizzaro and put him in the same cell as me."

"Did you already know him?"

Pasquale became evasive.

"Well . . . we worked together a few times."

Better not ask what kind of "work" they had done together.

"Go on."

"Inspector, you gotta believe me. This wasn't the same Peppi I used to know. He was changed. Before, he was always jokin' around, all friendly, laughing over the littlest bullshit. But now he was all silent and gloomy and nervous."

"Why?"

"He'd fallen in love."

"And that was the effect it had on him?"

"Yeah, 'cause he couldn't be without the girl. At night he would groan and call her name. I felt really bad for the poor guy! He was always holdin' up a picture of her, and now and then he'd kiss it. Then one day he let me see it. She was really a beautiful girl."

"How is it you could see the tattoo in the photo?"

"'Cause the picture was taken from behind, with the bottom cut off a little below the girl's shoulder blades and her head turned round. So you could see the butterfly real good."

"What did he tell you about her?"

"He said she was Russian, twenty-five years old, and she used to be a dancer."

"What was her name?"

"Zin, I think."

What kind of name was that? Perhaps a diminutive for Zinaida?

"What else did he tell you about her?"

"Nothing."

"Where can I find Cannizzaro?"

"How should I know, Inspector? I'm inside and he's out."

"Thanks, Pasquà. I hope they let you out soon. You've been very helpful."

Before leaving the prison, he asked the management office for the address of Peppi Cannizzaro. He lived in Montelusa, in a cross street off Via Bacchi-Bacchi. The inspector decided to go see him at once.

———

It was a four-story building. Cannizzaro lived on the third floor. Montalbano rang the doorbell, but nobody came to the door.

He rang a bit longer. Nothing. So he started knocking with his closed fist. Then he complemented the fist with a few kicks. He made so much noise that the door facing Cannizzaro's opened, and an infuriated elderly woman appeared.

"What's all this racket? My son is sleeping!"

"Well, signora, it's a bit late for sleeping."

"My son is a night watchman, you ignorant son of a bitch!"

"I'm sorry, I was looking for Cannizzaro."

"If he doesn't answer the door, it means he's not there."

"Do you know if he'll be back soon?"

"How should I know? I haven't seen Peppi going up or down the stairs for three days."

"Listen, signora, have you recently seen Peppi's girlfriend, who's called Zin?"

"What the hell do you care if I've seen her or not?"

"I'm Inspector Montalbano."

"D'you realize how much you're frightening me? You got me so scared I'm shittin' my pants!" said the old woman.

And she slammed the door in his face so hard that her poor night watchman of a son must surely have fallen out of bed.

There was no way to track down Cannizzaro.

He went back to the prison, and this time the warden made something of a fuss, but in the end she let herself be persuaded. Montalbano found himself with Pasquale in the same little room as before.

"What happened, Inspector?"

"I went to Cannizzaro's place, but he wasn't at home. The lady from the apartment across the landing says she hasn't seen him for three days."

"Zin wasn't there, either? Peppi told me he'd taken her home to live with him."

"She wasn't there, either. Any idea where I might find him?"

"No, Inspector. But maybe talking to somebody in here . . . Two of Peppi's friends are here . . . If I find anything out, I'll let you know."

He didn't arrive at the office till past midday, his nerves on edge from the heavy traffic he'd encountered on the way there. The moment he walked in, Catarella launched into a Greek choral lament.

"Ahh Chief Chief!"

"Wait. Is Fazio here?"

"He ain't here yet. Ahh Chief Chief!"

"Wait. What about Augello?"

"Him neither. Ahh Chief Chief!"

"Jeez, what a pain in the ass, Cat! What is it?"

"The c'mishner called! Twice, he called! An' he was rilly ousside himself, he was! An' the secon' time more than the foist!"

"What's he want?"

"He says as how you gotta drop everyting yiz about to

be doin' and go emergently right now to see 'im. God, you shoulda heard 'im yell! Wit' all doo respeck for the c'mishner, he was like 'e was outta his mine!"

What could the inspector possibly have done to put the commissioner in such a rage? Then he had a frightening thought. Want to bet it turned out that Picarella had indeed been kidnapped?

"Do me a favor, call Fazio on his cell phone and put him through to me on the office phone."

"Buuu . . . Chief, Chief, if you don't go there emergently, the c'mishner—"

"Just do as I say, Cat."

The moment he sat down, the phone rang.

"Fazio, where are you?"

"In Montelusa, Chief. Doing what you asked me to do."

"D'you find out anything about Mirabilis?"

"I'll tell you later."

Therefore there *was* something. He'd been right.

"Listen, Fazio, I've been called into the commissioner's office, and I wouldn't want . . . Is there any news about the Picarella kidnapping?"

"What news could there possibly be, Chief?"

"See you at four."

He hung up.

"Catarella? Call Inspector Augello on his cell."

"Straightaways, Chief. Count up to five . . . 'ere 'e is, Chief, I'll put 'im on."

"Mimì, where are you?"

"In Monterago. I've checked out the furniture works they've got here."

"Find anything?"

"Nothing. They make modern furniture without any gilding. Horrendous."

"Do you know by chance if there's any news about Picarella?"

"Why should there be any news about Picarella?"

"See you at four."

He went out, cursing the saints as he got in his car, and headed back up the road to Montelusa. It was a good thing the pleasant morning weather had held up. There wasn't a cloud in the sky.

"Hello, Montalbano."

"Hello, Dr. Lattes."

How was it possible that every time he went to the commissariat, the first person he ran into was always Dr. Lattes, known as Caffè-Lattes?

"How's the family?"

Lattes—the chief of the commissioner's cabinet—had long ago got it in his head that Montalbano was married with children, and there was no convincing him otherwise. Thus Montalbano's reply could only be:

"They're all fine, with thanks to the Blessed Virgin."

Lattes said nothing. Since "with thanks to the Blessed Virgin" was an expression he was very fond of, why hadn't he joined the inspector in giving thanks, as he normally would? And why hadn't he called him "dear inspector," as was his custom? Montalbano noticed that Lattes was less expansive than usual. He wondered whether the man's attitude was owing to the fact that the commissioner had called him in.

"Do you know the reason—"

"I haven't been informed."

Too quick to respond was the chief of the cabinet. Perhaps it was worth investigating.

"I'm afraid I've done something wrong," he muttered, assuming a contrite expression.

"I'm afraid you're right."

The tone was severe.

"So you know something but you don't want to tell me! Is it serious, Dr. Lattes?" Dr. Lattes nodded in confirmation. Montalbano continued to ham it up:

"Oh my God! I can't lose my position! I have a family to support! A real family! With all those children! Not one of those common-law arrangements like so many people have nowadays!"

Dr. Lattes looked carefully around. The usher was reading a newspaper. They were the only two people in the waiting room.

"Listen to me," he said brusquely. "Apparently you—"

At that moment the commissioner opened the door to his office.

"You mean he's still not here, that—"

Lattes had an instinctive reaction. Using both hands, he pushed Montalbano towards the commissioner and at the same time gave a little jump, to put some distance between himself and the inspector.

What, did he have the plague or something?

"He's here!" he yelled.

"I can see. Come in, Montalbano."

"Do you need me for anything?" Lattes asked.

"No!"

The door closed behind the inspector with the thud of a tombstone.

11

It had to be something very serious. So it was best not to start making wisecracks right off the bat with Bonetti-Alderighi. Or to give in to the desire to have it out with him and have the whole thing end in a blowup.

The commissioner went and settled into the armchair behind his desk, but made no sign to Montalbano to sit down. Which was in itself a confirmation of the gravity of the situation.

Bonetti-Alderighi sat there a good five minutes, staring at the inspector as if he'd never seen him before, and the conclusion of his examination was a disconsolate "Bah!" Montalbano expended half his energy reserves merely keeping still and silent and not flying into a rage.

"Would you explain to me how you get certain ideas into your head?" the commissioner finally began.

What ideas was he referring to? For caution's sake, it was probably best to play it safe.

"Look, Mr. Commissioner, sir, if you want to talk about Picarella's so-called kidnapping, I take full—"

"I don't give a damn about the Picarella kidnapping. But don't worry, we'll have plenty of opportunities to talk about that later."

So why, then?

All at once he remembered that fucking Piccolo file, when he had written back to the commissioner in poetry. Want to bet Bonetti-Alderighi, inspired by the Holy Spirit, had realized he was making fun of him by answering him in verse?

"Ah, I get it. You're referring to what I wrote when I said that Vigàta is not Licata, and Licata not Vigàta . . ."

The commissioner goggled his eyes.

"Are you insane? What is this, anyway? I know perfectly well that Vigàta is not Licata, and Licata is not Vigàta! Do you take me for an idiot? Listen, Montalbano, don't start in with your usual routine of playing dumb. I assure you this is really not the time for it!"

The inspector surrendered.

"All right, then, *you* tell me."

"Damn right I'll tell you! Will I ever! But please let me get something straight. Explain to me exactly what sort of enjoyment, what sovereign pleasure you experience in getting yourself and me into trouble?"

"No enjoyment or pleasure at all, believe me. And I assure you that when this happens, I don't do it intentionally."

"Are you telling me you don't do it on purpose?"

"Exactly."

"Then that's even worse!"

"Why?"

"Because it means that you act indiscriminately, without weighing the consequences of what you do."

Keep calm, Montalbano, keep calm. Count to three before you speak. Actually, count to ten.

"Have you lost your voice?"

"But what did I do?"

"What did you do?"

"Yes, what did I do?"

"Would you please explain to me why you went and stirred things up at Benevolence? Why? Would you be so kind as to tell me why?"

So that was what all the mystery was about.

All the same, how quick Cavaliere Piro was to go run and complain to the people in charge! And if the cavaliere was so quick to run for cover, want to bet that when the inspector had smelled a rat, he had smelled right?

"Do you even know who those people have behind them?" the commissioner continued.

"No, but I can easily imagine. Was it Monsignor Pisicchio who called you?"

"Not only the monsignor, but also the prefect, whose wife contributes very generously to that charitable association; and also the vice president of the region. Not to mention the provincial councillor for social welfare. As well as the municipal councillor. You have stuck your finger into a real hornet's nest, do you realize that?"

"Mr. Commissioner, sir, when I stuck my finger in it I didn't know yet that it was a hornet's nest. Actually, in appearance, it seemed like anything but a hornet's nest. All I did was ask a few questions of the person to whom Monsignor Pisicchio had referred me, a man by the name of Guglielmo Piro."

"Who claims that you used an insulting, inquisitorial tone after you burst in on him."

"Burst in on him? He himself gave me an appointment!"

"Could you at least tell me why you went and bothered this Monsignor Pisicchio and his association?"

With saintly patience Montalbano explained to him how he had come to investigate the association.

When the commissioner resumed speaking, his tone had changed slightly.

"It's a tremendous headache, you know."

"I agree. From our perspective, however, the moment we make a move on a case, we always run into a parliamentary deputy, priest, politico, or mafioso, who then form a daisy chain to protect the person likely to be under investigation."

"For heaven's sake, Montalbano, spare me your theories! In all honesty, do you really think there could be a connection between the charitable association and the murdered girl?"

"I stick to the facts. I had no choice but to go question the people at Benevolence, because two other girls with the same tattoo as the murder victim sought help from the association. You can't find a closer connection than that!"

"But do you think there's more?"

"Yes, but I haven't yet figured out if this 'more' really exists, and, if so, what it consists of."

"It's the fact that you say 'yet' that worries me."

"What do you mean?"

"How much more time 'yet' will you be investigating the association?"

How could he possibly know exactly how long it would take?

"I can't say with any certainty."

"Then I'll tell you myself. I'll give you four days and not one day more."

"And what if it's not enough?"

"You'll have to make do. And, during these four days, I advise you to proceed with the utmost caution."

"Don't worry, I won't spare the Vaseline."

Damn, it had slipped out!

"I wouldn't make wisecracks if I were you, because if I receive another complaint, you'll be the one to take it you-know-where, and without Vaseline! And if they object to your methods, I shall remove you from the case at once. And even if you eat humble pie at my feet, I will turn a deaf ear and say: You can't fool me twice!"

Hearing such a long string of clichés, Montalbano felt suddenly dizzy. A feeling of nausea came over him.

"In other words, Mr. Commissioner, if you break it, it's yours."

"I see that you understand me perfectly."

In the waiting room Lattes was talking to someone. But the moment he saw Montalbano come out of the commissioner's office, he rushed into the first open door he could find, and disappeared.

Clearly he didn't want any contact with Montalbano the outcast, the excommunicate, the stinking anticlerical who didn't deserve the beautiful family he had created with the Madonna's blessings.

It was getting late, and his hunger was eating him alive. Probably because of the effort he'd made to stay calm during his meeting with Bonetti-Alderighi.

"The fresh fish arrived today!" said Enzo the moment Montalbano walked into the trattoria.

He not only had a feast, but when it was over he took his customary walk out to the lighthouse. The fisherman was in his usual spot.

"I was wrong," he said. "It didn't last a week."

"So much the better. But will it start raining again?"

"Not right away."

As soon as he got to the flat rock, it occurred to him, for no apparent reason, that he had never sat down on it with

Livia. But would Livia have ever agreed to sit down on it? Today, for example, surely not.

"Can't you see that it's still wet?"

It was true. All the little pits and hollows on the rock still glistened with rainwater. If he sat on it, the seat of his trousers would become one dark wet spot. He remained standing, undecided.

Do as Livia would suggest, said Montalbano One.

Do what you want to do, said Montalbano Two.

Montalbano sat down on the rock.

Did you do it to spite Livia? asked Montalbano One.

Of course, replied Montalbano Two.

How is that spiting anyone? If Livia were here, then all right, but in the present circumstances . . . , said Montalbano One.

It doesn't matter if Livia is here or not, retorted Montalbano Two. *The point is to take a stand. That's the reality of it.*

"Could I say something?" Montalbano himself said at this point. "The only reality is that my trousers are now sopping wet."

"Ah, Chief! Mr. Gracezza called."

"What did he want?"

"He emergently wanted a talk to you poissonally in poisson. He said as how if you could call him 'cause he's at home anyways."

"I'll call him later."

Augello and Fazio were already in his office waiting for him.

"What have you got to tell me, Mimì?"

"What have I got to tell you? The other furniture works also makes modern furniture and doesn't use purpurin."

"And you, Fazio?"

"Can I use notes?"

"As long as you don't start reciting me any birth certificates."

"The Mirabilis Company of Montelusa has been in operation for about ten years and is properly incorporated. They're involved in buying—and then reselling or renting out—large buildings, such as hotels, office buildings, conference halls, industrial warehouses, things like that."

"So Mirabilis does *not* own the villa, as Piro claimed?"

"Piro spoke the truth. The villa does belong to Mirabilis, but it's an exception; they don't own any others. They bought it less than five years ago from the agency of Guglielmo Piro, who had bought it for a song from the Marchese Torretta, because it was falling into ruin."

"What a wonderful coincidence!" Montalbano exclaimed.

"What?"

"The Benevolence Association was set up five years ago, and immediately Mirabilis finds, through Piro, a villa made to measure and rents it to them. Were you able to find out how much they pay?"

"Seven thousand euros a month," replied Fazio.

"A pretty penny, twice the going rate in Montelusa. Did you get the names of the board of directors?"

"Of course," said Fazio, laughing.

"Why are you laughing?"

"You'll laugh, too, as soon as you hear one of the names. So, currently on the board of directors we have the chairman and managing director, Carlo Guarnera, and the associates Musumeci, Terranova, Blandino, and Piro."

"Piro?"

"Emanuele Piro, Chief."

"Is he a relative of—"

"He's Guglielmo's younger brother. Emanuele joined the board of directors two months before Mirabilis bought the villa. What, doesn't that make you laugh?"

"No."

"How about if I tell you that Emanuele Piro is considered a nitwit who spends his days popping blackheads and starts crying if the wind blows his kite away?"

"Shit!" said Mimì.

"Obviously Emanuele is a front man for his brother, the cavaliere," said Montalbano, who then started to laugh.

"And why are *you* laughing now?"

"Because, though it has nothing to do with our investigation, I just thought of another cavaliere who uses his younger brother as a front man for himself. It's become a widespread practice."

"What can we do?" asked Augello.

"What do you want to do, Mimì? There's nothing illegal about it. Or 'actionable,' as one says nowadays. Even a homicide, with these new laws, can prove 'unactionable.' Forget about it. That association, as I immediately realized, must be one giant pork barrel. And then some. But we have to proceed very carefully."

"What did the commissioner want you for?" asked Augello.

"Mimì, you're a subtle one. How did you know I went to talk to the people of Benevolence? Who told you?"

"I told him," Fazio cut in.

"And Cavaliere Piro raised the roof. The commissioner is willing to cover us for four days, then we're on our own."

"Would you please tell us what you found out?" asked Mimì.

Montalbano told them. And he concluded:

"Irina Ilych, Katya Lissenko, and Sonya Meyerev, all three were dancers from Schelkovo, all three had the same moth tattoo, and all were lodged for a certain period of time at the villa rented by the association. They showed up of their own accord and had not been persuaded to do so by Tommaso Lapis or Anna Degregorio. At least that's what Piro told me. And he added that they were very frightened when they arrived but hadn't told him why. But who knows if this story of them being scared is true or not? One week later, Sonya disappears. Katya goes to work as a home care assistant for Mr. Graceffa, but when she's no longer needed, she disappears, too. Irina instead goes to work as a maid at the house of my friend Ingrid, steals her jewels, and disappears in turn. But there's a fourth girl with the same tattoo. Her boyfriend, a hoodlum by the name of Peppi Cannizzaro, calls her Zin, which is perhaps short for Zinaida. This girl is the only one who didn't pass through Benevolence."

"Or maybe she did, and Piro didn't want to tell you," Mimì cut in.

"Right. In any case, Peppi Cannizzaro and Zin are also nowhere to be found."

"But how many more dancers from Schelkovo with a moth tattoo are still going to crop up in this affair?" asked Augello.

"I don't think there are any others aside from these four."

"Why not?"

"I don't know that to be true with any certainty. But . . . doesn't a moth have only four wings?"

"To conclude, the murdered girl can only have been either Sonya or Zin," said Fazio.

"Precisely," Montalbano approved.

"But why did they kill her?" Mimì wondered.

"I'm beginning to have an idea," said the inspector.

"Well, what are you waiting for?"

"It's the thinnest of threads, too vague, really."

"Well, tell us anyway!"

"Irina's a thief. Zin hooks up with a thief. Katya, on the other hand, confides to Graceffa that she wants to steer clear of a certain environment. And in fact she doesn't steal anything from Graceffa, even though she keeps phoning a certain Sonya."

"What are you getting at?"

"Let me finish, Mimì. Let's stop to think about Irina for a moment. She steals quite a few jewels. But she's a foreigner. How's she going to make contact with the local crime circuits where she can resell them? Who could she possibly have met in the short amount of time she's been in Montelusa?"

"Well, to venture a guess—" Mimì began.

"I haven't finished. Now let's take the girl who was murdered. Pasquano found black wool filaments inside her head. They can't be from a sweater or scarf. So I say, what if, at the moment she was killed, the girl was wearing a ski mask so she wouldn't be recognized?"

"You think she might have been caught in the act of committing a robbery?"

"Why not? Somebody catches her by surprise and shoots her. Haven't you heard about the wonderful new law on self-defense passed by our sovereign Parliament?"

"But wouldn't it have been better for the person who shot her to leave the girl's body right where it was, without going through all the hassle of stripping her and throwing her into the dump?" Fazio cut in.

"Of course," Montalbano admitted. "But I prefaced my statement by saying that my hypothesis was weak. If, however, we can prove that the murdered girl is Sonya, who is blond—I saw her passport photo—then my question to you is: Who did Red Riding Hood find in her grandmother's bed?"

"The wolf," said Mimì.

"Right. And the wolf is none other than the charitable association."

"Agreed. But how will we—"

"Fazio, what other news have you got for me about Guglielmo Piro?"

"I didn't have enough time, Chief."

Montalbano pulled a folded piece of paper out of his jacket pocket.

"This was given to me by Monsignor Pisicchio. It's got the names of everyone who works for the association. They're listed here by first and last names, address, and telephone number. That's not enough for me. I want to know everything about them, and I mean everything. Guglielmo Piro, Michelina Zicari, Tommaso Lapis, Anna Degregorio, Gerlando Cugno, and Stefania Rizzo. You can skip the telephone operator and the cleaning help. Split the work up between the two of you, but I want at least some information by noon tomorrow."

He phoned Graceffa without putting the call through the switchboard. The other picked up after one ring.

"Hello?"

"Signor Graceffa, Montalbano here."

"Ah, thank you, Doctor, I was waiting for your call!"

"Signor Graceffa, I'm not your doctor, I'm Inspector Montalbano."

"Yes, I know."

"What did you want to tell me?"

"Isn't it better if I come to your office, Doctor?"

It suddenly became clear to Montalbano. Graceffa's niece must be nearby, and the old man didn't want her to hear what he had to say.

"It's a delicate matter, isn't it?" the inspector asked in a conspiratorial tone.

"Yes."

"Could you come to the station right away?"

"Yes. Thank you."

Beniamino Graceffa walked into the inspector's office with the same attitude a Mazzinian activist must have had when he went to a secret meeting of la Giovine Italia.

"Would you let me make an urgent phone call?"

"Use this phone here."

"Dr. Marzilla? This is Beniamino Graceffa. Listen, if my niece Concetta calls, I'm on my way to your office. No, I'm not on my way to your office, but I want you to tell her that, please. Okay? Thanks."

"Does your niece keep tabs on you?" asked Montalbano.

"Every time I go out."

"Why?"

"She's worried I spend my money on whores."

Maybe young Concetta wasn't entirely wrong.

"What did you want to tell me?"

"I wanted to tell you that this morning I took the bus to Fiacca."

"For business?"

"What business? I'm retired! I went . . . iss a delicate matter."

"Don't tell me. Then why did you want to talk to me?"

136

"Because as I came out after taking care of that delicate matter, and went to catch the bus back home, I saw Katya."

Montalbano sat up in his chair.

"Are you sure it was her?"

"I'd bet my life on it."

"And did Katya see you?"

"No. She was standing there unlocking the front door of her building. Then she went in and shut the door behind her."

"Why didn't you call out to her and try to talk to her?"

"There wasn't any time. If I missed the bus, what was I gonna tell my niece?"

"Do you remember the street and number of this building?"

"Of course. Via Mario Alfano, number 14. It's a small, two-story house. Outside the front door is a plaque with the name 'Ettore Palmisano, Notary.' "

12

After Graceffa left, the inspector told Catarella he wanted to see Fazio and Mimì at once. But Augello was already gone. Apparently Beba had called him because the baby had a bellyache again.

Fazio listened carefully to the inspector's summary of developments and then asked:

"Should we go immediately to Fiacca?"

"I don't know."

Fazio glanced at his watch.

"If we leave right away, we'll definitely be there by eight-thirty, in Fiacca, that is," he said. "That's a good time. We might just find the notary at the table with his wife, as Katya is serving them supper."

"And what if Katya doesn't work evenings and therefore doesn't sleep at the notary's house at night but somewhere else?"

"We'll ask Palmisano to give us the address of where she sleeps, and then we'll go and talk to her."

"Assuming the notary knows the address. And assuming that Katya gave him the right one."

"Then let's phone Palmisano right now, let's talk to him, see what the situation is, and act accordingly."

The more determined Fazio seemed, the more Montalbano felt doubtful. But the truth of the matter—as he well knew—was that he had no desire whatsoever to tramp all the way to Fiacca that evening.

"And what if Katya answers?" he objected.

"I'll tell her that my name is Filippotti, and that I urgently need to speak with the notary. If the notary himself answers, so much the better."

"And what will you say to the notary?"

"I'll tell him who I am and ask him if Katya Lissenko sleeps at his house or if she's lodged somewhere else. If she's staying at his place, there's no problem; I'll tell him we'll be there in an hour and ask him to say nothing to the girl. If, on the other hand, the girl sleeps elsewhere, I'll ask him for the address. Did I pass the test you're giving me?"

"All right, go ahead and try. Call on the direct line and turn on the speakerphone."

Fazio looked up the number in the phone book and dialed.

"Hello?" answered an elderly woman.

Fazio looked baffled at the inspector, who gestured to him to keep talking.

"Is this . . . the Palmisano home?"

"Yes, but who is this?"

"Filippotti. Is the notary there?"

"He's not back yet. He went out for a walk. I can take a message, if you like; I'm his wife."

"No, thanks, have a good evening."

He hung up.

"Couldn't you make up some bullshit to find out if Katya was there or not . . . ?"

"Sorry, Chief, I got confused. I hadn't figured on the wife being there when I was studying for the exam."

"You know what? With this brilliant idea of calling them up, we may have created a problem," said Montalbano.

"Why?"

"I'm convinced that Katya knows everything, including the fact that one of her group of tattooed girls was murdered. She's scared to death and trying to hide."

"I realized that myself. But why do you think we've created a problem?"

"Because if Katya, as she's serving them dinner, hears the wife tell the notary that a certain Filippotti called and he says he doesn't know him, the girl might get suspicious and disappear again. But maybe that's an exaggerated concern."

"Yeah, I think so. What are we going to do?"

"Pick me up in a squad car at eight o'clock tomorrow morning, and we'll go to Fiacca."

"And what about those people at Benevolence whose names you gave me?"

"You can deal with them when we get back."

After eating Adelina's preparation of mullet and onions on the veranda, he went inside and sat down in front of the television.

The Free Channel's evening news program presented stories that seemed copied from stories of the day before and the day before that.

Actually, if one really thought about it, the television had been presenting the exact same news items for years; the only things that changed were the names: the names of the towns in which the events were occurring and the names of the people involved. But the substance was always the same.

In Giardina the mayor's car was set on fire (the previous morning it had been the car of the mayor of Spirotta).

In Montereale, a town councillor was arrested for auction tampering, graft, and corruption (the previous day a town councillor of Santa Maria had been arrested on the same charges).

In Montelusa there was a fire set by arsonists, probably owing to failure to pay protection money, at a shop that sold picture frames and paints (the previous evening arsonists had set fire to a linen shop in Torretta).

In Fela the charred remains of a farmer earlier convicted of collaborating with the Mafia were found in his car (the previous evening it had been the turn of an accountant from Cuculiana, likewise a collaborator, to be charred).

In the Vibera countryside the search for a mafioso on the run for seven years intensified (the previous day the search for another mafioso, on the run for only five years, had intensified in the Pozzolillo countryside).

In Roccabumera, carabinieri and criminal elements exchanged gunfire (the previous evening bullets had been exchanged in Bicaquino, but instead of the carabinieri it had been the police).

Fed up, Montalbano turned off the television, lolled about the house for an hour, then went to bed.

He started reading a book that had been praised by a newspaper that discovered a new masterpiece every other day.

The human body begins to decompose four minutes after death. What was once the vessel of life now undergoes the final metamorphosis. It begins to digest itself. Cells start to decompose from the inside. Tissues turn to liquid, then to gas.

Cursing the saints, he took the book and hurled it against the wall in front of him. How could anyone read a book like that before falling asleep? He turned off the light, but the moment he lay down, he felt uneasy. He was very uncomfortable. Had Adelina somehow not properly made the bed?

He got up, tightened the bottom sheet, folded it well under the mattress, and lay back down.

Nothing doing. He still felt uncomfortable.

Maybe it had nothing to do with the bed. Maybe the problem was himself, something in his head. What could it be? The first lines of that damned book which had upset him? Or had something come to mind while Fazio was phoning the notary? Perhaps it was a news item he had heard on television, something that prompted a half-formed idea, the shadow of a thought immediately forgotten as quickly as it had appeared. It took him a long time to fall asleep.

Fazio arrived at eight on the dot in his own car.

"Why didn't you come in a squad car?"

"Still no gasoline, Chief."

"You going to pay for the gas for this trip yourself?"

"Yessir. I'll turn in the receipt."

"Do they reimburse you right away?"

"It takes a few months. And sometimes they reimburse me, sometimes they don't."

"Why not?"

"Because they follow a specific criterion."

"Namely?"

"How they happen to feel."

"This time, give the receipt to me, and I'll take care of turning it in."

They sat there in silence. Neither felt like talking.

When they were already on the outskirts of Fiacca, Montalbano said:

"Call Catarella."

Fazio dialed the number, brought the cell phone to his ear as he was negotiating a curve, and suddenly found himself before a roadblock of carabinieri. He slammed on the brakes, cursing. A carabiniere leaned downed to the car window, gave him a long, severe look, shook his head, and said:

"Not only were you speeding, but you were also talking on the phone!"

"No, I—"

"Are you going to deny that you had your cell phone to your ear?"

"No, but I—"

"License and registration."

The carabiniere used only his fingertips to take the documents Fazio held out to him, as if he were afraid of catching some fatal disease.

"Of all the . . . ," said Fazio.

"The guy's got the face of someone who's going to make you dance a jig at the very least, if your papers aren't in order," Montalbano seconded him.

"Should I tell him we're with the police?" asked Fazio.

"Not even if they torture you," replied the inspector.

Another carabiniere circled around the car. He, too, leaned down to the window.

"Did you know that your left taillight is broken?"

"Oh, really? I hadn't noticed," said Fazio.

"Did you know?" Montalbano asked a moment later.

"Of course I knew. I noticed it this morning. But I couldn't very well take the time to have it changed, could I?"

The second carabiniere started whispering to the first. Who, for his part, began writing things on the clipboard he had been carrying under his arm until now.

"I'm sure to get a fine this time," Fazio muttered.

"Do you get reimbursed for your fines?"

"Are you kidding?"

Meanwhile, out of one of the carabinieri's two cars stepped a marshal, who began to approach.

"Goddammit!" Montalbano exclaimed.

"What is it?"

"Gimme a newspaper, gimme a newspaper!"

"I haven't got a newspaper!"

"Then a road map, quick!"

Fazio handed him a map, which Montalbano opened up completely, pretending to study it and practically covering his whole face. But then he heard a voice through the car window.

"Excuse me, you!"

He pretended not to have heard.

"I'm talking to you!" the voice repeated.

He had no choice but to lower the map.

"Inspector Montalbano!"

"Marshal Barberito!" replied the inspector, making a considerable effort to feign surprise and smile.

"What a pleasure to see you!"

"The pleasure's all mine, I assure you," said Montalbano, getting out of the car and shaking his hand.

He felt, at that moment, that he could be included in the *Guinness Book of World Records* as champion of hypocrisy.

"Headed anywhere interesting?"

"To Fiacca."

Meanwhile the other two carabinieri had come closer.

"For a case?"

"Yeah."

"Give the driver back his documents."

"But . . . ," said one of the carabinieri, who, upon realizing that the two were from the police, didn't want to give up his bone.

"No buts," commanded Marshal Barberito.

"Look, Marshal, if we're at fault, we have no problem with—" began Guinness champion Montalbano, assuming the air of someone superior to the petty matters of existence.

"You must be joking!" said Barberito, holding out his hand to him.

"Th-thanks," said Montalbano.

He could barely refrain from exploding with rage.

They drove off. After a long silence, Fazio made the only comment possible:

"They made monkeys out of us."

Right outside the gates of Fiacca, Fazio's cell phone rang.

"It's Catarella. What do I do, answer?"

"Answer," said Montalbano. "And let me hear, too."

"There's not going to be another roadblock, is there?"

"I don't think so. The carabinieri have even less gasoline than we do."

"Come as close you can."

The inspector brought his head right up next to Fazio's. But because of the potholes in the road, every now and then they knocked heads like two rams.

"Hello, Catarella, what is it?"

"Is the chief on the premises poissonally in poisson inside your car?"

"Yes. Go ahead and talk so he can hear you."

"Ah, I'm so touched! Jesus, I'm rilly, rilly touched!"

"Okay, Cat, try to calm down and talk."

"Ahh Chief Chief! Ahh Chief Chief! Ahh Chief Chief!"

"Is this a broken record or something?" asked Fazio, who

drove with his left hand while using his right hand to hold the cell phone within range of his ear and the inspector's.

"If he says 'Ahh Chief Chief' three times it must be something really serious," said Montalbano, feeling slightly worried.

"You gonna tell us what happened or not?" said Fazio.

"They found Picarella! Found 'im this morning! Passed on to a better life!"

"Shit!" exclaimed Fazio as the car swerved, provoking a pandemonium of screeching tires and horn blasts from cars, motorbikes, and trucks going in both directions.

"Holy fucking shit!" Montalbano hurled back.

Fazio dropped the cell phone to gain better control of the car.

"Pull over and stop," said Montalbano.

Fazio obeyed. They looked at each other.

"Shit!" said Fazio, reasserting the concept.

"So the kidnapping was for real!" said Montalbano, confused and bewildered. "It wasn't a put-on!"

"We were wrong about him, poor guy!" said Fazio.

"But why did they kill him without first asking for a ransom?" Montalbano wondered.

"Who knows?" muttered Fazio, who again repeated, in a soft, frightened voice: "Shit!"

"Call up Augello and pass me the phone."

Fazio picked up the cell phone and dialed the number.

"*The telephone of the person you are trying to reach . . .*," began the woman's recorded voice.

"He's got it turned off."

"*Matre santa*," said Montalbano. "Now if the commissioner kicks our asses and rakes us over the coals he'll be right!"

"And what am I gonna do with Signora Picarella? This is gonna turn out badly for all of us! The commissioner'll probably have us out on the street selling chickpeas and pumpkin seeds!" said Fazio, beginning to sweat.

The inspector, too, felt as if he was sweating. The matter was certainly bound to have serious, indeed grave, consequences.

"Call Catarella again and ask him if he knows where Augello is. We have to come up with a plan of common defense immediately."

Since they weren't moving, it was easier for Montalbano to listen.

"Hello, Cat? Do you know were Inspector Augello is?"

"Seeing as how Inspector Augello found hisself on the premises herein at the station when we got the news that the beforementioned Picarella was found, he bestook hisself to the Picarella house wherein to talk . . ." (*He went and faced the just-widowed Signora Picarella?* Montalbano thought. *Mimì's a brave man!*) ". . . with the same poisson," Catarella concluded.

Montalbano and Fazio looked at each other, speechless. Had they heard right? Had they really heard what they'd heard? If Picarella was dead, the same person with whom Mimì had gone to talk to could not humanly be Picarella. But Catarella had said "the same poisson." The question was: What did Catarella mean by "same"?

"Make him repeat it," said Montalbano, on the verge of a nervous breakdown.

Fazio spoke with the same caution one uses in talking to a raving madman.

"Listen, Cat. I'm going to ask you a question, and I want you to answer simply yes or no. Okay? Is that clear? Not one word more. Yes or no, all right?"

"Okay."

"Did Inspector Augello go talk to Mr. Picarella, the man who had been kidnapped?"

"All right," said Catarella.

Montalbano cursed, as did Fazio.

"You're supposed to answer yes or no, dammit!"

"Yes!"

"Then why did you say Picarella was dead?"

"I din't."

"What? Inspector Montalbano heard it, too, when you said that Picarella had passed on to a better life!"

"Oh, yeah, I said that, sure."

"But why did you say that?"

"But in't it true? Before, when 'e was still kidnapped, 'is life was bad, an' now 'e's free so 'e got a better life."

"I—one of these days, I swear, I'm gonna shoot that guy," said Fazio, turning off his phone.

"But the coup de grâce will be mine," said Montalbano.

"Shall we turn back?" asked Fazio.

"No. Mimì was right to go immediately to Picarella's. We, for our part, will continue on our way. But at the first bar we see, we're going to stop and have a nip of cognac. We need it. This journey has been too full of adventure."

When they arrived in Fiacca it was already past eleven.

They found Via Mario Alfano at once, a broad street with little traffic. The front door of the house was closed, but under the plaque was a buzzer with an intercom. Montalbano rang. A moment later, a woman's voice answered.

"Who is it?"

"Chief Inspector Montalbano of Vigàta here."

"What do you want?"

"I'd like to speak with the notary."

"He's busy. Please go into the waiting room. You'll be called when it's your turn."

They went into an anteroom with two doors on the left-hand wall, over one of which was a sign with the words "Waiting Room," as one used to see in train stations. On the right were two other doors, over one of which was a sign saying "Office"; under this, in smaller letters, the words "Please do not enter."

At the far end of the room was a staircase leading upstairs, which must certainly be where the notary and his wife lived.

Fazio opened the door to the waiting room, stuck his head inside, pulled it back out, and reclosed the door.

"There's about ten people waiting in there."

"As soon as someone comes out of the office, we'll send word to the notary," said Montalbano.

A good ten minutes later, the inspector lost patience.

"Fazio, try going up a few stairs and calling the wife."

Fazio climbed three steps and starting calling in a low voice.

"Signora! Signora Palmisano!"

"She's not gonna hear you if you say it like that!"

"Signora Palmisano!" Fazio repeated a little more loudly. No answer.

"I think you should go upstairs and tell the wife we want to talk to her."

"And what if she gets scared at the mere sight of me?"

"Try not to frighten her."

Fazio resumed climbing the stairs so cautiously that if Signora Palmisano did see him she was certain to take him for a burglar. Which would unleash further pandemonium to go with all the other pandemonium of the morning.

13

While waiting, could he smoke a cigarette? Montalbano took a look around and saw no signs forbidding it. To be honest, he didn't see any ashtrays, either.

What to do? He decided to light up a cigarette and, after smoking it, to put the butt in his jacket pocket. He had just taken the first puff when Fazio appeared at the top of the stairs:

"Chief, come on up."

He extinguished the cigarette and slipped it into his pocket. When he was beside him, Fazio whispered:

"She's a very nice lady."

They'd barely taken two steps when Fazio stopped, took a deep breath, flared his nostrils, and said:

"I smell something."

"Metaphorically speaking?" asked Montalbano.

"No, sir, speaking for real."

Montalbano realized he hadn't fully extinguished the cigarette butt and that his jacket was burning. But since he couldn't very well present himself to the lady in his shirt-sleeves, he limited himself, cursing, to slapping the pocket of his jacket to put out the budding fire.

Ernesta Palmisano, sixtyish, well dressed, and without a hair out of place, showed them into an elegant living room.

Montalbano was immediately dazzled by five or six bottles by Morandi and two women bathing by Fausto Pirandello.

"Do you like them?"

"They're magnificent. Very beautiful."

"Then later I'll show you a Tosi and a Carrà. They're in my husband's private study. Can I get you anything?"

Fazio and Montalbano looked at each other and understood at once. It was their chance to see Katya.

"Yes," they answered in unison.

"Coffee?"

"Yes, please," replied the well-trained little chorus.

"Unfortunately, I have to go make it myself because today the maid—"

"Whaa . . . ?" Montalbano yelled, leaping to his feet.

"Wha'd the maid do?" Fazio completed his question, also standing up.

Signora Palmisano got scared.

"Oh my God! What did I say?"

"Please forgive me, signora," said the inspector, trying hard to remain calm. "Is your maid a young Russian named Katya Lissenko?"

"Yes," replied the woman, bewildered.

"What did she do?" asked the little chorus.

"She didn't come today."

More than sit back down, Montalbano and Fazio collapsed into their armchairs. They had gone to all this trouble for nothing. Signora Palmisano returned and also sat back down, completely forgetting about the coffee.

"Did she phone to tell you she couldn't come?" asked the inspector.

"No. But this has never happened before. She has never

missed a day. She's always been very conscientious, punctual, and well organized . . . If only they were all like her!"

"How long has she been in your service?"

"For three months."

So she had moved to Fiacca right after working for Graceffa in Vigàta.

"At what time was she supposed to come into work?"

"At eight."

"Why haven't you phoned her to find out why—"

"I called her around nine, but nobody answered. There probably wasn't anyone at home."

"Where does she live?"

"She rented a small room from the widow Bellini, in Via Attilio Regolo 30."

"How did she end up working for you?"

"She was recommended to us by Don Antonio, the parish priest at the church just down the street. But could you tell me why all the questions about Katya? Has she done anything wrong?"

"Not that we know of," said the inspector. "We're looking for her because she might be able to give us some very important information about a case we're working on, involving the murder of a Russian girl. Have you heard about it?"

"No. When I hear news of murders on television, I immediately change the channel."

"You're absolutely right. What kind of a person is Katya?"

"She's a very serene girl, a normal girl. I wouldn't exactly call her lighthearted, or sad, for that matter. Every now and then she seems absent . . . distracted . . . as if following some unpleasant train of thought."

"Signora, I want you to think carefully before answering. Did you notice anything different in Katya in the last few days? I mean the period from Monday evening up to and including last night."

"Yes," Signora Palmisano said at once, without needing to think it over.

"What did you notice?"

"When she came in Tuesday morning, she was very pale and her hands were shaking a little. I asked her what was wrong, and she replied that she'd received a phone call from her hometown . . . Schelkovo?"

"Yes."

"And that she'd been given some bad news."

"Did she say what?"

"No. And I didn't insist, because I could see she didn't want to talk about it."

"Did you notice anything else?"

"I'll say! Yesterday morning, when she got back from the post office, where my husband had sent her to mail some registered letters, she seemed quite upset. When I asked her why, she said she didn't feel well. She said she'd sort of fainted and thought it must be because of the bad news, which she couldn't get over. That was why I wasn't too surprised when she didn't show up this morning. I had promised myself that if I couldn't get her on the phone, I would go to see her this afternoon."

Without a doubt, contrary to what Graceffa said, Katya had definitely seen and recognized him. And she was afraid that he might return and get her into trouble.

Signora Palmisano, who was a real lady, had no more questions. The inspector instead asked, as he was standing up:

"Would you show me the other paintings?"

"Of course."

There wasn't a single law book in the notary's private study. The shelves were full of novels of the highest quality.

The landscape by Tosi was superb, but when standing before Carrà's seascape, Montalbano was moved almost to tears.

When leaving the Palmisano home, he noticed that the insufficiently extinguished cigarette butt had made a hole in his jacket pocket. Still taken by the beauty of the Carrà painting, he didn't even feel like cursing.

But why, in 2006, would a mayor still want to name a street after Atilius Regulus? The mysteries of toponymy. At number 30 Via Attilio Regolo they found a run-down, six-story building without an elevator, and the widow Bellini naturally lived on the sixth floor. They climbed the stairs slowly, yet were still out of breath when they arrived at her door.

"Whoozzat?"

The voice of an old woman.

"Signora Bellini?"

"Yes. Whattya want?"

Montalbano had an inspiration: If he told her he was a police inspector, she was liable not to open for anything, not even cannon fire. The elderly, however, always allowed swindlers into their homes without any problem.

"Are you retired, signora?"

"Yes, I scrape by."

"We're here to make you an interesting offer."

Fazio gave him a look of alarm.

The door opened as far as the chain would permit. Signora Bellini looked them up and down as Montalbano and Fazio tried to assume as angelic an air as they could. The widow decided to remove the chain.

"Come in."

The apartment was clean, the old furniture in the small

living room so polished that it sparkled. All three politely sat down. Montalbano regretted not having a briefcase from which to pull out some papers.

"Take notes," Montalbano ordered Fazio.

His assistant took a notepad and pen out of his pocket.

"You ask the questions," the inspector continued.

Fazio's eyes glistened with contentment. Anything to do with people's vital statistics were like drugs to a drug addict for him.

"First name and maiden name."

"Rosalia Mangione."

"Day, month, year, and place of birth."

"September the eighth, 1930, in Lampedusa. But . . ."

"Yes, signora?" said Montalbano.

"Could you tell me who gave you my name?"

Montalbano stuck a big smile on his face, all teeth, like Sylvester the Cat.

"Katya told us about you."

"Oh."

"Is she here? We'd like to say hi to her."

"Katya's not here. When she came home lass night, she packed up her bags, paid me the rent, and left."

Montalbano and Fazio stood up simultaneously.

"Did she tell you where she was going?" asked the inspector.

"No."

"Monday evening, did Katya receive a telephone call from Russia?"

"Not a chance."

"What makes you say that? Doesn't Katya have a cell phone?"

"Sure. But she's not the type to be talkin' to the whole world."

"Do you have a television?"

"Yes . . . but . . ."

"But what?"

"I haven't paid the subscription for five years."

"Don't worry about it. Did you hear about the murdered girl who was found in an illegal dump?"

"The one with the butterfly? Yes."

"Did Katya know about it?"

"She was with me when they reported it on TV."

"Let's go," said Montalbano.

The old woman ran after them.

"What was the offer?"

"We'll be back this afternoon, and we'll make you our offer then," said Fazio.

Montalbano realized at once that Don Antonio was going to be difficult.

Fiftyish, stocky, muscular, and taciturn, he had hands that looked like sledgehammers. In a corner of the sacristy, the inspector espied a pair of boxing gloves hanging on the wall.

"You a boxer?"

"Now and then."

"Excuse me, Father, but was it you who put the Palmisano family on to Katya Lissenko?"

"Yes."

"And who, in turn, was it who put you on to her?"

"I don't remember."

"Let me try to help you. Perhaps it was the Benevolence Association of Monsignor Pisicchio?"

"I have no dealings with Monsignor Pisicchio or his association."

Was there not a note of disdain in his voice? Fazio must have heard it, too, because he shot a glance at the inspector.

"You don't remember at all?"

"No."

"And there's no way that, with a little effort . . . ?"

"No. Why are you looking for her? Has she done anything wrong?"

"No," said Fazio.

"We only want to question her concerning some things she may know about," Montalbano clarified.

"I see."

But the priest didn't ask what these "things" might be. Either he wasn't curious or he knew perfectly well what these "things" were. But weren't priests supposed to be curious by profession?

"Why did you come looking for her here?"

"Because she never returned to the Palmisanos' and left her own lodgings all of a sudden. So we thought that Katya, having turned to you once before for help—"

"You were mistaken."

"Father, I have reason to believe that this girl could be in grave danger. Maybe even mortal danger. Therefore, whatever information you—"

"Would you believe me if I told you I haven't seen Katya for the last ten days or so?"

"No," said Montalbano.

The priest looked meaningfully at the boxing gloves.

"If you want to submit to God's judgment and fight it out, I'm ready," said the inspector, hoping that Don Antonio wouldn't take him seriously.

And, in fact, for the first time, the priest laughed.

"And then you'll charge me with resisting arrest and assaulting a police officer? Listen, Inspector, I like you. Along with all her bad luck, Katya, who's a good girl, also had some good luck. After deciding not to have anything more to do with the Benevolence people, she has met the right people, and they've been able to help her. Leave me your telephone number, and if I have any news of Katya, I'll let you know."

Montalbano wrote down some numbers for him, including that of his home phone, then asked:

"Do you know why Katya no longer wanted to have anything to do with Monsignor Pisicchio's association?"

"Yes."

"Could you tell me?"

"No."

"Why not?"

"Because it was told to me during confession."

They left Fiacca.

"Do you think we'll ever hear back from the priest?"

"I think so. After he's consulted with Katya. Because it's Don Antonio—and I would bet my family jewels on it—who saw to finding a safe hiding place for Katya. Maybe even in his own home."

"So you would say that, all things considered, our trip was not entirely in vain?"

"Exactly. I actually think we have established indirect contact with Katya."

"Do you know what time it is? We won't be back in Vigàta till three-thirty or so," said Fazio.

At that hour, they were sure to find nothing left to eat at Enzo's.

"If the carabinieri stop us again, we won't get back till five. And I'm hungry."

"Me, too," Fazio seconded him.

Montalbano saw a sign at a crossroads.

THE WINGS OF THE SPHINX

"Turn left here. We're gonna go to Caltabellotta."

"What for?"

"There used to be a good restaurant there."

Fazio turned onto the road indicated.

A passage from a history lesson came back to Montalbano, and he recited it aloud, with eyes closed:

"The Peace of Caltabellotta, signed on August 31, 1302, put an end to the War of the Vespers. Frederick II of Aragon was recognized as King of Trinacria and pledged to marry Eleanor, sister of Robert of Anjou."

He stopped.

"So?" asked Fazio. "How'd it end up?"

"How did what end up?"

"Did Frederick keep his pledge? Did he marry Eleanor?"

"I don't remember."

⬛

"Poach a head of cauliflower in salted water, remove it when still slightly firm, and chop it into large chunks. Then season it in a skillet after you have sautéed a small onion, thinly sliced, in olive oil in the same pan. In another pan, fry up a piece of fresh sausage, and the moment it turns golden, cut it into small disks no more than an inch wide, removing the skin. Add the cauliflower to the pan with the sausage bits and oil, adding a few potatoes sliced into thin, transparent disks, some chopped black olives, salt, and spices. Stir this assortment well. Knead some leavened bread dough into a broad, flat disk and mold this into a cake tin with a tall rim; fill this with the mixture and cover with another round sheet of dough, kneading the edges together. Spread lard over the upper parts and put the tin into a very hot oven. Remove it as soon as it turns golden brown (but this will take half an hour or so)."

This was the recipe for *'mpanata di maiali* that the inspector asked the cook to dictate to him after he and Fazio had finished licking it off their fingers. For a first course, they had gone light: *risu alla siciliana*, that is, rice seasoned with the flavors of wine, vinegar, salted anchovies, olive oil, tomatoes, lemon juice, salt, hot pepper, marjoram, basil, and dried black *passuluna* olives.

They were dishes that called for wine, and the call did not go unanswered.

When they stepped back out into the open air, Montalbano regretted that he couldn't take his customary walk to the lighthouse at the end of the jetty.

"Listen, Fazio, let's have a little walk. We can go as far as the castle, then come back and pick up the car."

"Good idea, Chief. That way the smell of the wine we drank should evaporate a little. If the carabinieri stop us now, they'll throw us in jail for DUI."

The walk helped a bit. As they were getting back into the car, Fazio saw a man raising the shutter over the front of a books and paper shop.

"Would you excuse me a minute, Chief?"

"What do you need to do?"

"This evening my wife and I have to go to the house of a friend whose little boy is turning four. I want to buy him a set of colored chalks for his birthday."

He returned with a small box, laid this down on the dashboard, and they set off.

At the first curve, the box slid off the dashboard and fell to the floor near Montalbano's feet. As he was picking it up, he was wondering if colored chalks already existed when he was a little kid or if all chalk was white. He was about to put the box back in the same place when his eye fell on some very fine print on one side: "Arena Color Works—Montelusa."

He didn't know there was a color works in Montelusa. One that, moreover, retailed color products.

It was hard to think clearly with all the wine he had in his body. His thoughts were sort of all jumbled together and almost impossible to disentangle.

Where was he? Ah yes: the colors sold in colors shops. So what? Some discovery! *Congratulations, Insp*— Wait a minute! What had he heard last night on television? *C'mon, Montalbà, think hard, it might be really important!* Searching for a fugitive, the arrest of a town councillor . . . Aha! A fire, probably arson, at a shop that sold frames and paints in Montelusa. So that was the news that hadn't let him fall asleep! Where can one find purpurin in considerable quantities? Either where it is made or where it is sold. Not where it is used, because the people who use it need only a little tiny bit of it. He'd got it all wrong.

"Asshole!" he said, giving himself a powerful slap in the forehead.

The car swerved.

"Do we wanna do a repeat of this morning?" asked Fazio.

"Sorry."

"Who you upset at?"

"With myself, first of all. And second, with you and Augello."

"Why?"

"Because we're never going to find purpurin in significant quantities in furniture factories or restoration workshops, but only in places where it's produced or sold. Last night on the news I heard that there was a fire in a store that sold paints. I'd like to drop in there right now. Call one of our people in Montelusa and get the phone number and address of the proprietor."

14

One could not say Carlo Di Nardo was secretive about his work.

He welcomed Montalbano into his office at Montelusa Central with open arms. After all, they'd been fellow travelers and had always been fond of each other.

"To what do I owe the pleasure?"

Montalbano explained what he wanted.

"Here in Montelusa you have only to look in three places: the Arena Color Works, which supplies half of Sicily, the Disberna sisters' shop, and Costantino Morabito's store, or what remains of it. Now, I think I've understood that you believe the girl fell when she was shot and got purpurin all over herself. Is that right?"

"That's right."

"Then I would rule out that either of the Disberna sisters could have shot any living thing, even an ant. And there's only the two of them, who are both around seventy, looking after the store, with the help of a niece who's about fifty. They didn't do it, I assure you. The color factory, on the other hand, is big, and you probably ought to have a look there."

"Can't you tell me anything about Morabito's store?"

"I've saved that for last. First of all, it was clearly a case of arson, there's no doubt about that. Except that a different method was used in this case."

"Namely?"

"You know how the shops of people who don't pay the protection racket usually get torched? Very rarely do the arsonists ever enter the shop. They normally limit themselves to throwing gasoline through an open window or pouring it under the front shutter or door. In ninety percent of the cases where the arsonist actually goes inside, he ends up getting more or less severely burnt."

"So here the fire was started from the inside?"

"Exactly. And none of the metal shutters, doors, or windows had been forced. Mind you, this is also the opinion of Engineer Ragusano of the Fire Brigade."

"So, all things considered, you would lean towards a hypothesis implicating Morabito himself in the deed?"

"My, how diplomatic you've become in your old age, Montalbà! Even Locascio, the insurance man, thinks Morabito did it."

"For the insurance money?"

"That's what he thinks."

"And you don't?"

"Morabito's financial position is pretty solid. If he set fire to his own store, there must be another reason. I had promised myself I would try to find out tomorrow, but then you arrived. What are you going to do now?"

"I want to go have a look at Morabito's store."

"No problem. I'll go with you. You coming, too, Fazio?"

The store that sold paints wasn't really, strictly speaking, a paints store. It was rather unimaginatively called Immaginazione and was a kind of supermarket where one could buy a great variety of things for the home, from bathroom tiles and rugs to ashtrays and light fixtures. The very large paints department was the part of the store that had been destroyed by fire, and very little of it remained. Anyone wishing to paint their bedroom straw-yellow with little green checks and their dining room fire-engine red could find everything they needed here; just as anyone devoted to painting pictures could choose from thousands of tubes of oil paint, tempera, and acrylics.

In this section of the store was a staircase that led to the apartment in which Costantino Morabito, the proprietor, lived. Naturally one could also enter the flat from a front door that gave onto the street; the internal staircase was merely a convenience that allowed Morabito to open and close the store from the inside.

Di Nardo answered all the questions the inspector asked him, which were many.

"I want to talk to Morabito," Montalbano said as they returned to Montelusa Central.

"No problem," Di Nardo said again. "He's moved in with his sister, since his place may be unsafe. The firemen need to do a safety check."

"Speaking of firemen, who controls this neighborhood? Who runs the protection racket?"

"The Stellino brothers. Who, in my opinion, are pissed off about this fire, which will be blamed on them even though they probably had nothing to do with it."

"That might be a good starting point for making Morabito nervous. Where can I talk to him?"

"In my office. I have to go do something else. I'll put Detective Sanfilippo at your disposal; he knows everything."

"If Morabito wasn't hard up for cash, why would he set fire to his store?" asked Fazio, as soon as they were alone. "Inspector

Di Nardo," he continued, "told us he wasn't married, doesn't gamble, hasn't got any girlfriends, he's not a big spender but just the opposite, a tightwad, and he hasn't got any debts . . . Why rule out arson by the protection racket?"

"I once saw an American movie, a comedy," Montalbano said distractedly, "about a guy who brings a whore home with him, taking advantage of the fact that his wife has gone to spend the night at her mother's place. When she starts getting ready to leave, three hours before the wife is supposed to be back, the whore can't find her panties. They look and look, to no avail. The whore leaves. And the man, realizing that sooner or later his wife is gonna find those goddamn panties, goes and sets fire to the house. Doesn't that seem like a good reason to you?"

"But Morabito isn't married!" said Fazio.

"It's not the same thing, of course. But I was wondering: What if the fire was set to hide something else that couldn't be found?"

"Like what?"

"Like an empty shell."

"What are we gonna do?"

"Tell Sanfilippo to bring in Morabito. And I'm warning you now: Give me a lot of rope, 'cause I'm really gonna ham it up."

Costantino Morabito was a man of about fifty who was sloppily dressed, carelessly shaven, with wild hair and dark bags under his eyes. He was extremely nervous and moved in fits and starts. He sat down on the edge of the chair, pulled a handkerchief out of his pocket, and held it in his hands.

"It was a nasty blow, eh?" Montalbano asked after introducing himself.

"Everything ruined! Everything! The smoke got soot all

over everything, even the stuff in the other departments, and ruined it all! The damage is incalculable! I'm finished!"

"But in your misfortune you were lucky."

"What do you mean, lucky?"

"Lucky to be still alive."

"Oh, yes! With the help of San Gerlando! It was a real miracle, Mr. Inspector! The flames very nearly engulfed the upstairs where I was and roasted me alive!"

"Listen, who first realized there was a fire?"

"I did. I noticed a strong burning smell, and—"

"I smell it, too," Montalbano interrupted him.

"Right now?" asked Morabito, confused.

"Right now."

"Where?"

"It's coming from you. How odd!"

He got up, walked around the desk, went up to Morabito, bent down, bringing his nose to about a couple of inches away, and began sniffing him from the hair to the chest.

"Come and smell for yourself."

Fazio got up, stood on the other side of Morabito, and started doing the same as the inspector.

Flummoxed, Morabito froze.

"You can smell it a little, can't you?"

"Yeah," said Fazio.

"But I washed!" Morabito protested.

"It takes a while for it to go away, you know."

They returned to their places.

"You can continue, Mr. Morabito."

"I smelled something burning, so I opened the door to the stairs and the smoke poured in and I started choking. So I called the firemen and they came right away. Do you know how easily paints can catch fire?"

"What were you doing?"

"I was going to bed. It was past midnight. I'd been watching TV . . ."

"What were you watching?"

"I don't remember."

"Do you remember the channel?"

"No. But . . ."

"Go on, go on."

"I'm sorry, Inspector, but I've already told the whole story to the local police, the fire chief, the insurance people . . . What's this got to do with you?"

"I and my colleague Fazio are part of a special new team appointed by the commissioner. Very special. We deal in cases of arson that can be attributed to failure to pay the protection racket."

The inspector then stood up and started yelling.

"We can't go on this way! Honest businessmen like yourself must never again be subjected to the Caudine Forks imposed by the Mafia! We've waited forty years, and that's enough!"

He sat down, congratulating himself for both the Caudine Forks and the quotation of Mussolini. Fazio looked at him in admiration.

Costantino Morabito, shaken first by the smelling, then by the yelling, swallowed the lie like fresh water and became much more nervous.

"I . . . I would rule that out."

"You would rule what out?"

"The f-failure to pay . . ."

"You pay the racket regularly?"

"No . . . it's got nothing to do with paying or not paying. I am certain that the cause of the fire is not what you think."

"It's not? And what do *you* think is the cause?"

"I don't think it was arson."

"So what was it, then?"

"Maybe a short circuit."

"Before summoning you here, I went and had a long talk with Engineer Ragusano of the Fire Brigade. He's ruled out any short circuits."

"Why?"

"Because the point where the fire started has been located, and there's nothing there that has anything to do with electricity."

"Then it must have been spontaneous combustion."

"Ragusano rules that out, too, because of the temperature. And he has some questions."

"He didn't ask me any."

"He hasn't yet, but he will."

The moment called for a slightly sinister chortle, which the inspector executed to perfection. This elicited another admiring glance from Fazio and a disconcerted stare from Morabito.

"Oh, will he ever!" he continued, following with another Mephistophelian chortle. "Want to hear one?"

"All right, let's hear one," said Morabito, wiping the glistening sweat from his brow.

"The fire started in a specific spot, at the foot of the internal staircase. Where there should not have been any inflammable material. But the firemen indeed found some right there. Ragusano told me these materials had been piled up, in fact, as if to form a little pyre. Who put them there?"

"How should I know?" replied Morabito. "When I closed the store, there wasn't anything at the foot of the stairs."

"Care to venture a guess?"

"What do you want me to say? They were probably put there by whoever started the fire."

"Right. But that raises another question: How did the arsonist get in there?"

"How should I know?"

"The store's two rolling metal shutters had not been forced. The windows were all found closed. How did he get inside?"

The handkerchief with which Morabito was wiping his brow was soaked.

"He might've used some kind of timing device," he said. "Something he left at the foot of the stairs before the store closed."

"Did you close up the store from the outside?"

"No. Why would I do that? I closed it up the way I've always done."

"Which is?"

"From the inside."

"And how did you return to your apartment?"

"How else? I went up the inside stairs."

"In the dark?"

Morabito's sweat had now soaked through his jacket as well. He had two dark stains under the armpits.

"Whattya mean, in the dark? I turned on the light."

"Come on! If you turned on the light, you would have to have seen the timing device. Didn't you see it?"

"Of course I didn't see it!"

"So I shall make a note that you admit—"

Morabito lurched so severely in his chair that he nearly fell.

"What . . . what do I admit? I haven't admitted anything!"

"I'm sorry. Let's proceed in an orderly fashion. At first you maintained that the fire might have been started by a short circuit or spontaneous combustion. Correct?"

"Yes."

"But if you now come out with this idea that it was a timing device, it means you're admitting that arson is a possibility, after all. Makes sense, no?"

Morabito didn't answer. An ever so slight tremor began to run through his body.

"Listen, Morabito, I'll meet you halfway. I can see you're having trouble. Shall we set aside this idea of a timing device, since, in any case, no trace of one was ever found?"

Morabito nodded, to say yes. Apparently he was unable to utter a word.

"Very well. Nix the timing device. According to Ragusano," Montalbano continued, "that little sort of pyre created for the purpose was generously doused in gasoline, after which, all it took was one match . . . You must admit, it's very strange!"

"What's very strange?"

"That the firebug didn't catch fire himself! Ha ha! That's a good one! Ah, so good! You know, like the Lumière brothers' *l'arroseur arrosé*, or the doctor who gets a taste of his own medicine!"

And he laughed, stamping his feet on the floor and slapping the desktop loudly.

Morabito stared at him, frightened and bug-eyed. Perhaps he was beginning to wonder if he wasn't dealing with an imbecile or a raving lunatic. What the hell was the guy talking about?

"Unless . . ."

Sudden change of expression. Brow furrowed, eyes pensive, mouth slightly twisted.

"Unless?" Morabito asked almost breathlessly.

"Unless the firebug wasn't already on the stairs. He makes the little pile, goes up the stairs, and throws the lighted match,

or whatever it was, down from above, since by now he's beyond the reach of the flames. But in that case . . ."

Suspense. Pause. Squinty facial expression because an idea
was taking form in his brain.

". . . in that case?" Morabito exhaled.

"In that case, to get out of harm's way, the firebug had no
other choice but to enter your apartment. Did you see him?"

"Who?" asked Morabito, completely at a loss.

"The firebug."

"How on earth—?!"

"Are you sure?"

"If I say—"

Montalbano raised his hand.

"Stop!"

And he started staring at the upper left-hand corner of the
room. Then he whispered to himself:

"Yes . . . yes . . . yes . . ."

He looked back down at Morabito:

"Do you know I'm starting to have an idea?"

"An idea . . . of what?"

"That you not only saw the arsonist, but you even recognized him and you don't want to tell us."

"Wh-why wouldn't . . ."

"Because you're afraid. And you're afraid because the arsonist was one of the Stellino brothers, the mafiosi who control your neighborhood."

Morabito stood straight up, staggered, and had to sit back
down.

"For heaven's sake! For the love of God! The Stellinos had
nothing to do with this! I swear it!"

"That's what you say. And since you say it . . . You know
what? I'm starting to have another idea."

Morabito threw up his hands, resigned.

"Do you have enemies?"

"Enemies, me? No."

"And yet one would think that somebody wanted to . . . what's the expression? It's not coming to me . . . Fazio, help me out."

"To do him a bad turn?" Fazio offered.

"Yes, that's it! Or we could even say they wanted to set you up! Don't you think, Mr. Morabito?"

"I . . . I . . . don't understand . . ."

"But it's all so simple! Somebody who wants to harm you sets fire to your store so that the blame will fall on the Stellino brothers."

"Could be," said Morabito, grasping at Montalbano's words.

"Think so? I'm so happy that you agree, you know! Really happy! Because, you see, there's somebody else who thinks it was arson: Mr. Locascio, the insurance assessor."

"Well, I'm not surprised! Those people are always looking for excuses not to pay!" said Morabito, a bit revived.

"Locascio, however, doesn't think it has to do with protection money."

"No? And what's he think?"

"You want me to tell you? You really want me to? He thinks it was you yourself who set the fire, so you could collect on the insurance."

"That goddamn son of a bitch! Why would I need any insurance money? My business is doing great! Go and ask the banks, why don't you!"

"But my colleague Inspector Di Nardo, who interrogated you, thinks differently."

"Differently from who?"

"From Locascio, naturally. He firmly believes it was about failure to pay the racket. And that was why he asked us to help out. He wants to pin this fire on the Stellino family, who control the area your store is in. Try to be brave, Mr. Morabito. One word from you, and we can put the Stellinos behind bars!"

"We're back to the Stellinos? But they've got nothing do with this!"

"Are you sure?"

"Absolutely. And anyway, even if they did, one word from me, and they'll kill me!"

"Especially if they had nothing to do with the fire, as you have repeatedly stated."

"Listen, Inspector, you keep talking and talking and I don't understand anything anymore!"

"Are you getting tired? Shall we take a break?"

"Yes."

"You going to report me?"

"Me, report you? Wh-why would I do that?"

"If I smoke a cigarette, I mean. It's not allowed in here."

Morabito shrugged his shoulders.

15

The inspector took his time smoking the cigarette, and since he saw no ashtrays anywhere, he snuffed it out against the heel of one shoe and put the butt in his jacket pocket. After all, he already had a nice hole in it, and one hole more or less wasn't going to make any difference.

For the whole time of his smoke, nobody said a word. Morabito sat there with his elbows on his knees and his head in his hands. Fazio pretended he was writing down the proceedings. Only after putting out the butt did Montalbano notice.

"What on earth are you doing?"

"I was making notes of the interrogation."

"What interrogation? We're having an informal conversation among friends. Otherwise Mr. Morabito would have every right to demand that a lawyer witness the proceedings, and we would have to call one for him. Speaking of which, do you want one?"

"One what?"

"A lawyer."

"Why would I want a lawyer?"

"You never know. But if you're so certain about everything that you think you don't need one, so much the better. Do remember, however, that I made you this offer. Feel a little better now?"

Morabito shrugged again, without even looking at him.

"Then we'll resume. I believe we came to a full stop—that is, the fact that we have to set aside the Stellinos, at least for this go-round. Do you agree?"

"I agree, I agree."

"So you've always paid your protection money on time?"

Morabito didn't answer.

"Listen, if you admit paying the racket, the whole matter will remain between the three of us. It'll never leave this room. But if you deny it, and I later find out that you paid, I might get pissed off. And that would be so much the worse for you, 'cause when I get pissed off . . . well, you tell him, Fazio."

"You're better off dead," Fazio said darkly.

"Got that? So think it over carefully. Let me ask you again. Do you pay your protection money regularly?"

"Y-yes."

"So you've got nothing to worry about, from that angle."

"Yes."

"However . . ."

"However?"

"That would no longer be the case if I, say, went and told the Stellino brothers that you had accused them. Don't you think they would take it badly and immediately come and demand an explanation from you?"

Costantino Morabito leapt so far out of his chair that he nearly fell to the floor.

"B-but wh-why would you go and do something so stupid as that? I thought we agreed that the Stellinos had no part in this!"

"Then start talkin' and tell me who and what's got a part in this!" the inspector suddenly yelled, slamming his open hand on the desk and making even Fazio jump.

"I don't know! I don't know!" Morabito yelled in turn.

And he started crying bitterly. All of a sudden. Like a small, frightened child.

Montalbano noticed a packet of paper tissues on the table, pulled one out, and handed it to him. With Morabito's own handkerchief one could have mopped the floor by this point.

"Mr. Morabito, why are you acting this way? I'm surprised at you! You seem like such a sensible man. Is it my fault? Is it something I said? Fazio, help me out a minute. What did I say?"

"He might've got upset 'cause you raised your voice," said Fazio, poker-faced.

"Ah, I didn't realize it, I'm so sorry. Sometimes it just happens, I can't help it."

Morabito wouldn't stop crying. Montalbano stood up halfway, leaned towards him, and shouted:

"What's seven times eight? Six times seven? Eight times six? Answer me quick, for chrissake!"

Morabito, still lost in his tears, was so surprised by the questions that he turned and gawked at the inspector.

"You see? He's calmed down! I've always said it: in moments of crisis, all you gotta do is review your multiplication tables, and it'll all blow over!"

He sat back down, a satisfied expression on his face.

"Listen, can I get you anything?"

"A little . . . a little water."

"Let's get him some water," the inspector said to Fazio. Then, turning around to Morabito: "We'll be right back."

They went out into the corridor.

"One more push and he'll cave in," said Montalbano.

"Was it him who set fire to the store?"

"I no longer have any doubt. And he's scared that the Stellinos will get blamed for it. I almost feel sorry for the guy: He's like a rat being pursued by two starving cats: the Mafia and the law!"

"But why would he do it?"

"Remember that film I told you about? To hide something that could have really big consequences."

"Such as?"

"What if he was the one who shot and killed the girl?"

"That's possible, too. But earlier, you mentioned an empty shell. What if Morabito happened to use a revolver?"

"I'll ask him straightaway. Go get him his water; we don't want to leave him any time to think. And don't forget: Be ready to step in, 'cause I'm about to play my aces."

Morabito downed the whole glass in one gulp. His throat must have been parched, scorched worse than his store.

"Tell me something. Do you own a firearm?" the inspector resumed.

Morabito, not expecting the sudden change of subject, gave a start. The effort he had to make to reply was plain to see. Montalbano realized he was on the right track.

"Yes."

"Rifle? Carbine? Pistol? Revolver?"

"Revolver."

"Registered?"

"Yes."

"What caliber?"

"I dunno. But it's big."

"Where do you keep it?"

"At home. In the drawer of my nightstand."

"After we've finished here, we're gonna go to your place."

"Why?"

"I want to see your revolver."

"Why?"

"I'm sorry, but you've got to stop this constantly asking why, why, why."

Morabito's sweat had soaked through the front of his shirt.

"You feel hot? Want another Kleenex?"

"Yes."

"Have you used your revolver recently?" asked Fazio, who had suddenly grasped the inspector's intentions.

"No. Why should I have used it?"

"How should we know? You're the one's supposed to tell us. Anyway, we'll know immediately whether you fired it recently or not."

The tissue in Morabito's hands ripped.

"H-how?"

"There are so many ways. Listen, anybody ever try to rob your place?"

"Well, yes. Every now and then, somebody comes into the store—"

"That's shoplifting, not robbery."

"I don't—"

"I was referring to robbery at your home."

"N-no."

"Never?" Montalbano cut in, having taken a break.

"Never."

"Do you keep a lot of money at home?"

"The day's receipts, which I deposit at the bank the following day."

"Why not deposit it in a night safe?"

"Because one night two shop owners were assaulted on the way to making a deposit."

"So you don't deposit your Friday and Saturday receipts till Monday morning?"

"R-right."

"Therefore one can assume that on Saturday evenings there's always a large sum of money in your apartment?"

"Yes."

"Where do you usually keep the money? Do you have a safe?"

"No, I keep it in a desk drawer."

"Do you live alone?"

"Yes."

"Who does your housekeeping for you?"

"Well ... you see ... since I have a cleaning company come do the store, we made an agreement ..."

The effort of having to talk so much had worn him out. He started panting, as though out of breath.

"Mr. Morabito, I can see that you're tired, and so I'd like to wrap things up. You can answer my questions with a simple yes or no. So you've ruled out arson?"

"Y-yes."

"Therefore you've ruled out any involvement on the part of the Stellinos?"

"Yes."

"The fire was accidental, in your opinion?"

"Y-yes."

"Very well. Then there remains only one more thing for me to do."

"Wh-what's that?"

"Summon you to appear here tomorrow morning at nine o'clock."

"Again? Why?"

"For a confrontation between witnesses."

"Wha-what witnesses?

"The Stellino brothers. I'm going to have them arrested this very evening."

Great big tears started rolling down Morabito's face again. His chin was trembling. The tremor in his body had become so visible that he looked as though he had an electrical current running through him.

"Mr. Morabito, I can see that this fire has been a very trying experience for you. I don't want to tire you out any further. Very well. I think I've finished for this evening. Now we go to your place to have a look at that revolver."

"But . . . we . . . can't!"

"Why not?"

"The Fire Brigade put—"

"Don't worry, we'll get their permission. Did you come here in your car?"

"No."

"But you've got one?"

"Y-yes."

"Where do you keep it?"

"In a gagagarage adjajajacent to the stostore."

"Has it got a big trunk?"

"Pretty big."

"Can't you be more precise than that? No? Let me give you an example. Is it big enough to hold a body?"

"But . . . what . . ."

"Don't get upset. There's no reason. Later we'll go have a look, at your car, that is. At the trunk, in particular. Fazio, before we leave, do you have any questions?"

The inspector prayed to God that Fazio would make the right move.

And Fazio, realizing that the inspector had passed him the ball, kicked it straight at the goal.

"I beg your pardon, but do you sell purpurin?"

He scored. Morabito stood up, spun halfway around himself, and fell to the floor like an empty sack. Fazio lifted him bodily and put him back in the chair, but no sooner was he sitting than he slid back down. A rag doll.

"Just leave him there. Call Sanfilippo and tell him to have Di Nardo come here at once," said Montalbano. "This moron most certainly killed the girl. Too bad!"

"Why too bad?"

"Because now the investigation goes over to Di Nardo, and Di Nardo will pass it on to Homicide. Territorial jurisdiction."

"So from this moment on, we're out of the picture?"

"Completely. In fact, you know what I say? I say I'm gonna call a taxi and go straight home to Marinella. I'll see you in the morning and you can tell me the rest of the story."

But he already knew the rest of the story and didn't need to wait till the following morning to find out. He played it out in his head as he was driving back to Vigàta.

One Saturday night Morabito is awakened by a noise. He pricks up his ears and is convinced there is a burglar in the house. So he opens the drawer of the nightstand, grabs his revolver, and quietly gets out of bed. And he sees that the burglar, having come in through the front door by using a skeleton key or something similar, is trying to open the desk drawer in which the proceeds of the previous two days are kept. The burglar, however, hears him and flees.

Most certainly the thief has somehow learned the layout of the flat and runs down the stairs that lead to the store. He had probably noticed, when reconnoitering the premises before entering the house, that the window in the paints section was open. In a flash he's in that part of the store, climbs up some shelving to reach the window, which is high, but then slips and falls straight into the little bags of purpurin, breaking a few of them open. When he turns around to see how far behind his pursuer is, Morabito shoots him.

The proprietor probably didn't mean to kill him, but the shot was right on target. The bullet, however, must have somehow moved the black wool ski mask covering the person's face, and thus Morabito realizes that the burglar is a woman.

And he loses his head.

It's true that with the new law on self-defense, he should get off without any problem, but—he wonders—does the law also apply if the thief is a woman? And, what's more, an unarmed woman?

As his initial moment of fright passes, he starts to think rationally.

And he begins to glimpse a way out. Since nobody heard the shot, wouldn't it be better to take himself out of the picture? To have nothing to do with it all?

He continues to think about it all night and the following day, Sunday. And he arrives at what he thinks is the right decision.

He strips the corpse and washes it, because the upper parts of the body are soiled with purpurin. Then he places it naked in the trunk of his car. This presents no problem because the garage communicates with the interior of the store, and therefore nobody can see him.

In the middle of the night between Sunday and Monday, he gets in his car and unloads the body at the Salsetto.

And there you have it.

But why, a few days later, did he decide that it was best to set fire to his business?

That was indeed something he would have to wait for Fazio to tell him in the morning.

When he got back to Marinella he was in such a dark mood that he didn't even want to eat.

He felt disappointed by the outcome of the case.

An idiotic crime committed by an idiot. On the other hand, how many intelligent homicides had he come across that had been committed by people with brains in their skulls? In his entire career, he could count them on one hand. Okay, but this last one was even stupider than the norm.

And once they had proof that Morabito had killed the girl, would Di Nardo, or the chief of Homicide, take things any further? Would they manage at least to give the murder victim a name? Or, once they realized that the case was in no way as simple as it seemed, would they simply withdraw?

And wasn't it his duty to inform his colleagues as to just how far he had gone in his investigation?

Because by this point there was no longer any doubt that at least two of the Russian girls with the sphinx moth tattoo were thieves. And it was proved that three of these girls had been associated with Benevolence.

Benevolence, therefore, was starting to look like pretty dangerous terrain, a veritable minefield when you came right down to it. Would Di Nardo, or someone in his place, feel like running the risk of being blown to bits? How many politicians with powerful connections in Rome, and all of them, whether of the right or left, with their wheels greased by priests, would "take the field" in defense of Monsignor Pisicchio and Benevolence? And would the public prosecutor have the courage to fulfill his responsibilities? After all, it took only a handful of questions to Cavaliere Piro to unleash a deluge of phone calls of protest to the commissioner.

Better not get any bright ideas. Sit tight. Leave the initiative to Di Nardo. If the commissioner's office started making noise and asking questions about the investigation he had conducted up to that point, he would tell them everything he had to tell. Otherwise, zip it, Montalbano, and stand pat.

As he sat out on the veranda, smoking and sipping whisky on a night that seemed made to dispel bad thoughts, the combination of disappointment and mild anger he had felt when he realized that the investigation had slipped out his hands began to dissolve.

Ah, well. It wasn't the first time this had happened to him.

Meanwhile, there was a positive side to all this, namely that he now had several trouble-free days ahead of him. Yes, he could take advantage of them to—

To do what? Montalbano One suddenly asked. *Would you please tell me exactly what you know how to do other than your job? You eat, shit, sleep, read a few novels, and every now and then you go to the movies. And that's it. You don't like to travel, you don't go in for sports, you have no hobbies, and when you come right down to it, you don't even have any friends with whom to spend a few hours . . .*

What is this bullshit, anyway? Montalbano Two intervened polemically. *He goes for longer swims than an Olympic champion, and you're telling me he doesn't go in for sports?*

Swimming doesn't count. What counts are genuine, serious interests, the kind that enrich and give meaning to a man's life.

Oh, yeah? Give me one example of these "interests"! Garden-

ing? *Collecting stamps? Discussing with friends whether Juventus deserved the championship more than Milan?"*

Would you let me finish? said Montalbano, butting in. *I was simply saying that I could take advantage of the free days ahead to have Livia come down. And you know what I say to you two? I'm going to pick up the phone and call her right now.*

He got up, went into the house, grabbed the telephone, dialed the number, and, at the first ring, hung up.

No, when he really thought about it, he wasn't exactly free at the moment.

The business of Picarella's disappearance was still hanging. It had completely slipped his mind. How had it turned out? Had he admitted to faking it or not? The inspector looked at his watch. Too late to phone Mimì. He might wake up the kid and trigger a revolution.

Perhaps it was best to wait till the following evening to call Livia, when he would be absolutely, or relatively, certain not to have any more hassles distracting him. He winced at the thought that a piddling matter like the Picarella disappearance could so affect his life. And so he made himself a solemn vow: By the evening of the following day, he would prove that Picarella had staged the whole thing and send the guy to jail for simulating a crime. Immediately after which he would call Livia.

He went to bed and slept six hours straight.

16

Almost straight, that is. Because he had a strange dream, after
which he briefly woke up before going back to sleep.

He was with Livia in the Bahamas (he knew it was the
Bahamas, even though he was certain at the same time that he
had never been there before). They were on a beach utterly
jam-packed with people, all in bathing suits: gorgeous topless
women in G-strings, youths like the boy in *Death in Venice*, fat
potbellied men, cuddling gays, lifeguards who were all muscle,
like the ones in American movies. Livia, too, was in her bathing suit. He, however, was not. He was all dressed up, and even
wearing a tie.

"Couldn't we have gone to a less crowded beach?"

"This is the least crowded one on the whole island. Why
don't you take your clothes off?"

"I forgot to bring my swimsuit."

"But you can buy one right here! See that airplane down
there? They sell everything there: swimsuits, towels, bathing
caps . . ."

There was an airplane parked on the beach with people all
around it, buying things.

"I left my wallet in the hotel room."

"You find every possible excuse not to go in the water!
Well, I'll show you!"

Suddenly they were no longer in the Bahamas.

Now they were in the bathroom of somebody's house, and Livia was his aunt while still being Livia.

"No, you're not going to school until you get undressed and take your bath!"

As he was taking his clothes off, feeling a little embarrassed, his Aunt Livia stared at a large black stain over his heart.

"What's this?"

"I dunno."

"How did you get that?"

"Dunno."

"Well, wash it off and call me before you get dressed, so I can check. And don't come out of the tub until that stain is gone."

Try as he might to wash it off, rubbing with soap and scrubbing with the sponge, the stain wouldn't go away. In despair, he started crying.

⬛

He opened his eyes and saw Adelina before him with a cup of coffee, the very aroma of which was restorative.

"D'I do right, signore? Maybe you wannata sleep s'more?"

"What time is it?"

"Almos' nine."

He got up, took a shower, got dressed, and went into the kitchen.

"Signore, I wannata tell you thet early this a mornin' I gotta phone call from the lawyer for my boy Pasquali, who you went a see yesterday in jail. The lawyer tol' me thet my boy tol' him to tell me an address thet I'm a sposto tell to you."

Montalbano felt slightly dizzy trying to follow the meaning of Adelina's last sentence.

"And what's this address?"

"Iss Via Palermo 16, in Gallotta.

It must be the address where Peppi Cannizzaro was living. Apparently he'd moved with Zin from Montelusa to Gallotta. But at this point it didn't matter anymore. The investigation was no longer his concern.

"When are they going to let him go home?"

"Mebbe in a coupla days."

"Thank him for the address. And gimme another cup of coffee, while we're at it."

"Ah Chief Chief! I hadda go all day yisterday witout seein' yiz!"

"Did you miss me? You're gonna see so much of me the next few days, you'll probably get sick of me."

"I never get sick o' you, Chief!"

A proper declaration of love. Uttered by anyone else, it would have been, at the very least, embarrassing.

"Who's here?"

"Everyone's here, Chief."

"Send me Augello and Fazio."

They were in the middle of an intense discussion when they arrived.

"Congratulations," said Mimì. "Fazio told me your performance with Morabito yesterday was one of your best."

"In all modesty . . . Listen, Fazio, don't tell me anything of what Morabito said. There's only one thing I want to know: why he set fire to his store."

"It was Ragonese's fault."

"The editorialist at TeleVigàta?"

"You bet. The day after the body was found, Ragonese,

discussing on TV the murder of the girl with no name—that's what he calls this investigation, the 'case of the corpse with no name'—"

"Sounds like the title of a movie," said Mimì.

"A B movie," added Montalbano.

"—revealed a detail mentioned by Pasquano."

"The purpurin?"

"No, sir, Pasquano didn't talk about the purpurin. But he did mention that the shot had blown away the girl's upper teeth. And so Morabito thought some of the teeth must be scattered around the spot where he killed her. As soon as he closed up the store, he spent the night looking for them but never found them. The cleaning team was supposed to come the next day, but he invented an excuse and told them not to come. And he continued to look, but to no avail. Finally, nearly out of his mind, he decided to torch his store."

"He should get off pretty easy," Montalbano commented.

"I don't think so," said Fazio. "The prosecutor was beside himself. Concealment and desecration of a corpse, arson—"

"Did Di Nardo by any chance tell you if he intended to get in touch with me to find out how far we'd got with the case?"

"No, but he couldn't stop singing your praises to the prosecutor. Aside from that—"

"Good. And you, Mimì, what'd you do with Picarella?"

"What do you think? The guy's an even better actor than you. I found him lying down, with his wife beside him, comforting him and holding his hand. Dr. Fasulo was also there, having just paid a house call and finding him in a 'deranged' mental state. I did manage, however, to ask Picarella a question: Could he please show me his passport?"

"Good for you, Mimì!"

"Thanks. He said the kidnappers had confiscated his passport."

"Of course! He could never show you the passport with the visits to Cuba stamped on it! He said 'kidnappers'?"

"Yes. Said there were two of 'em, even though Mrs. Picarella claims she only saw one."

"Did you talk about the photograph?"

"Of course. Both he and his wife covered me with insults and curses. They didn't come right out and say that it was a fake made by us, but they came close."

"So you think it's going to be a long, drawn-out affair with Picarella."

"Afraid so. Picarella will hold the line more because of his wife than for our sake. Bear in mind that it's the wife who has the money; he's pretty poor on his own. If his wife leaves him, he'll find himself crazy and broke. But at the moment we haven't got anything on him, except a highly contestable photograph."

"What are you going to do next?"

"In the meantime, I'm going to go back there with Fazio this afternoon at three. The prosecutor will also be there for formal questioning. And as concerns those names you gave me—"

"The ones from Benevolence? Forget about it, Mimì. Haven't you realized yet that we're out of the loop? Can I suggest a few things that you should ask Picarella in the presence of the prosecutor?"

"Go ahead."

"The prosecutor, naturally, will try to get details about the kidnapping: where they hid him, how they treated him, that sort of crap. And you can be sure Picarella will be very well prepared for such questions. You, instead, should ask him, first:

Do you have any idea why the kidnappers never demanded a ransom? Second: And if you weren't kidnapped for money, what other reason could there be? Third: Who might have known that you had withdrawn a large sum of money and were keeping it at home for only one night, the very night when you were kidnapped?"

"Those sound like three good questions to me."

"How many wood warehouses does Picarella have?" he asked Fazio.

"Two."

"Give me the addresses. Do we have a list of all the people who work at them?"

"Yup."

"Go get it. But first tell me something: In Picarella's absence, who kept the warehouses running?"

"Ragioniere Crapanzano."

"What have you got in mind?" Mimì asked him as Fazio went off to fetch the lists.

"I have an idea."

"Could I have a little preview?"

"Mimì, Picarella had one or two accomplices, right? Accomplices who ran, and are still running, the risk of prosecution. What I mean is that there are certain things people do out of friendship or for money. Didn't you and Fazio say that Picarella didn't have any close friends?"

"That's right, he's a lone wolf. He stays in his den and only goes out to hunt women."

"Which means he probably paid a high price to the accomplice or accomplices he needed to stage the kidnapping. I want to start looking for them among the men who work for him."

"Here are the lists," said Fazio, entering.

"Good. Now, I don't want any journalists talking to Picarella. I mean it. A total press blackout. We'll meet back up at nightfall."

"Ragioniere Crapanzano? Inspector Montalbano here."

"At your service, Inspector."

"Mr. Crapanzano, no doubt you're aware of the happy outcome of Mr. Picarella's kidnapping, for which we must eternally thank the Lord?"

"Of course, of course! We even toasted to celebrate! And we're considering holding a Mass to give thanks."

"Good for you! I think we can say, then, that his troubles are over, but somebody else's have only begun."

"Somebody else?" asked Crapanzano, concerned.

"Why, the person who kidnapped him, of course. We didn't make any moves earlier because we were afraid to put Mr. Picarella in danger. Now, however, our hands are no longer tied."

A great big lie, though plausible.

"What can I do for you?"

"Well, Ragioniere, aside from yourself, how many people work at the warehouse in Via Bellini?"

"Five. One clerk and four warehousers."

"And how many at the warehouse in Via Matteotti?"

"Also five."

"Good."

He looked at Fazio's lists. It tallied.

"In one hour, at the latest, I want to see all the employees together in your warehouse."

"But it'll be nearly one o'clock! We need to close for lunch!"

"That's precisely the point. You reopen at four, no? I need barely an hour, at the most. I won't make any of you miss lunch. And, that way, you won't have to keep your warehouses closed beyond the usual hours."

"Well, when you put it like that . . ."

Fazio's lists were very fussy: Not limiting himself to first name, last name, address, and telephone number, he also wrote down, for each employee, whether or not he was married, what vices he had, what criminal offenses, if any . . .

If Fazio, thought the inspector, hadn't been Sicilian but Russian at the time of the KGB, he would have had a brilliant career. Perhaps to the point of becoming prime minister, as had now become the custom there, in times of democracy.

When he arrived at the warehouse, they were all there.

Ragioniere Crapanzano, who looked to be in his sixties, introduced to him the firm's other *ragioniere*, a young man in his thirties named Filippo Strano, who managed the warehouse in Via Matteotti, as well as the fiftyish Signorina Ernestina Pica, accountant. There were only four chairs, and the inspector and the three clerks sat in them.

The warehousers, on the other hand, took their places on two wooden boards resting on top of other boards. Crapanzano introduced them all, from left to right.

Montalbano began to speak.

"I am sure Ragioniere Crapanzano has already told you who I am and why I wanted to see you all. We can't lose another minute in our pursuit of the dangerous criminals who kidnapped Mr. Picarella. I beg your pardon for asking you to come here during your break. But I think you'll understand that the real investigation of the case begins now. Poor Mr.

Picarella hasn't been able to say much yet, given the truly disturbing condition he finds himself in at the moment."

"Is he unwell?" Crapanzano ventured to ask.

Montalbano answered in masterly mime. He spread his arms, raised his eyes to the heavens, and shook his head several times.

"Very unwell. He can hardly speak."

"Poor man!" said Signorina Pica, the accountant, wiping away a tear.

"And this," Montalbano continued, "because he was severely beaten, day and night, during the duration of his confinement. That's what he told us. Kicked, punched, bludgeoned. Abused and humiliated in every way imaginable. And for no reason."

"Poor, poor man!" the accountant repeated.

"His jailers showed no pity. And such behavior aggravates their position. I believe the public prosecutor plans to charge them with attempted murder. We shall be implacable with them!"

Was it really going to be so easy? No sooner had he begun talking about the abuses to which Picarella was subjected, making them up on the spot, than the third warehouseman from the left, the fortyish Salvatore Spallitta, first made a face of utter befuddlement, then began to look quite afraid.

Montalbano looked down at one of the lists, which he'd held in his hand all the while. Spallitta worked at the Via Matteotti warehouse, and Fazio described him as a drug addict and occasional dealer.

Since he was already improvising his performance, he decided to keep it up.

"But there's more. And I ask you to pay close attention. No ransom was ever demanded for the liberation of Mr. Picarella. So why was he kidnapped? The answer to this question is very simple: To keep him away from his workplace for a while. For what reason? Because during that time, at one of his warehouses, or both, something was supposed to happen, without his knowledge, something he might have noticed had he been present."

"But ... nothing happened here during that time!" said Crapanzano.

Montalbano prayed to the Blessed Baby Jesus in heaven that something, anything at all, had happened at the other warehouse. And he looked straight at Filippo Strano.

"Nothing at our warehouse, either. Apart from a large shipment of lumber ... "

"From where?"

"From the Ukraine."

Montalbano chortled sardonically. He pulled it off well.

"And you call that nothing?"

"But why, if I may ask?"

"I'm sure *I* know why."

Ragioniere Strano fell silent, worried.

"Is the wood still in the warehouse?" the inspector continued.

"No. It was already reserved, so we—"

"Didn't waste any time, eh?"

Strano looked over at Crapanzano as if asking for help.

"Care to tell us why this wood was so special?" Crapanzano asked gruffly.

"Because some of the boards were hollow and contained narcotics," the inspector shot back.

Everyone present seemed to suffer a collective stroke simultaneously. Spallitta took it especially hard, turning pale as a corpse.

"This, mind you, is the assumption of the Narcotics unit. But they usually know what they're talking about."

The warehouse was quieter than a tomb.

"I don't want to take up any more of your time. Starting tomorrow, you will be called in, one by one, for questioning. Our interrogations will be long and thorough. A few agents from Narcotics will also be present. However—and this is why I wanted to meet with you—if, in the meantime, any of you thinks of anything, you can reach me by telephone. Good-bye, and thank you."

He stood up and went out, leaving them all in a daze.

At Enzo's he ate as ravenously as if he hadn't had a decent meal for years. Afterwards, seeing the kind of day it was, he took his usual stroll out to the lighthouse.

"What kind of weather we got coming?" he asked the angler.

"Good."

He sat down on the flat rock. But he didn't want to think about anything. He felt empty inside. He spent half an hour busting the balls of a crab that was trying to climb up a rock. Every time the creature progressed a couple of inches, he sent it back to its starting point with the flick of a twig.

Here you are again! said Montalbano One. *Aren't you ashamed of yourself? Look what's become of you! Toying with a crab!*

Would you leave him alone? intervened Montalbano Two. *What, is there some law against passing the time however one pleases? Did he do a good job this morning or not?*

Ah, imagine the effort! He must be dead tired!

To punish himself—since, at bottom, Montalbano One was right—as soon as he got back to the office he started signing the mountain of papers piled up on his desk.

At a few minutes past six, the phone rang.

"Chief, that'd be a Mr. Mallitta."

"Ask him what his name is."

"Chief, I jess tol' you what 'is name is."

"Ask him anyway."

The inspector heard some muttering in the background.

"I's wrong, Chief. 'Is name is Spalitta."

He was one *l* short, but the inspector was satisfied, perfection not being of this world.

"Put him on."

"I can't, seeing as how 'e's 'ere onna premisses."

"All right, then, send him in."

He felt absolutely certain that he would be able to call Livia that same evening. He had kept his solemn promise.

Spallitta looked like he was suffering from an attack of malaria.

"Do you have something to tell me?"

"Yessir. Since I've had a couple a minor drug convictions, I's scared o' you gettin' me mixed up in this."

"Mixed up in what, excuse me?"

"This business of the wood with the drugs inside. I swear I din't know nothin' about this and I still don't know nothin'!"

"Well, then, if your conscience is clear, what are you afraid of?"

"The fact is, that . . ."

". . . that your conscience isn't exactly clear, right?"

Spallitta dropped his head and said nothing.

"How much did Picarella give you to help him stage the kidnapping?"

"Five hundred euros. But, I swear, he tol' me it was all a joke! He needed to disappear for a week because he promised some whore he'd take her to Cuba. So why'd you feed us that bullshit about him gettin' beat up 'n' all? I always treated 'im just like he asked, I kep' 'im hidden at my brother's place in the country, every day I brought him food, cigarettes, newspapers ... An' now he wants to finish me off, the goddamn son of a bitch!"

There was a knock at the door, and Augello entered. Seeing that the inspector was busy, he made as if to leave.

"No, no, Mimì, come in. You dropped in at just the right moment. Have a seat. How'd the interrogation go?"

Augello had a moment of hesitation, given the stranger's presence. He decided to answer without mentioning any names.

"Not bad. I'd say in another couple of days, max, he's gonna crack."

"I'd say sooner. Oh, in case you haven't already met, this is Mr. Spallitta. He's the man who helped Picarella get kidnapped. You can continue talking here."

He stood up.

"And where are you going?" asked Mimì, a little flustered.

"To Marinella. I have to make an important phone call. See you tomorrow."

17

"How are you feeling?"

"A little better, thanks. And you?"

"Not bad, thanks."

"How's the weather there?"

"Good. How about up there?"

"Unstable."

How can two people spend years and years together and still be reduced to talking to each other like strangers? Wouldn't it be better to exchange a few obscenities and insults? And maybe even a few pushes and shoves, and a cuff to the head?

Montalbano felt a malignant rage against the situation in which he and Livia had come to find themselves. Whether it was his fault or Livia's fault no longer mattered. What mattered was for them to talk to each other a long time, eye to eye, to clear everything up and extract themselves, in one way or another, from the quicksands in which they were slowly sinking.

"Still got the same thing in mind?"

"What thing?"

"To come down here if—"

"Of course."

"Well, I wanted to let you know that I've managed to get myself three or four totally free days."

"Fine."

Was that it? Not *Oh how wonderful, I'm so happy*? What a shower of enthusiasm! Hadn't he kept his word? *I'll phone you as soon as I have a few free days*, he had promised her. He had raced home to Marinella to give her the good news, and this was her way of saying thanks?

"So, whenever you feel like it . . ."

"As far as I'm concerned, I could even come tomorrow morning," she quickly replied.

Which meant that she had already packed her bag and been waiting at home as long as possible for his phone call. And it also meant that her behavior showed not a lack of enthusiasm, as he had thought, but that she was carefully weighing every word she said, afraid that she might in some way let the intensity of her emotions show.

"Excellent. I'll come pick you up at Punta Raisi."

"No need to bother."

"Why not?"

"Because something might suddenly come up for you, and I don't think I could stand waiting for you and not have you come. For my own peace of mind, I would rather take the bus."

"But, Livia, I told you I'm totally free!"

"What does it cost you to let me—"

"But I told you there's no problem whatsoever! Come on, what time do you think you'll get in?"

"On the usual midday flight."

"I'll be there at noon."

"Listen, don't get mad, but . . ."

"But what?"

"I don't want us to stay in Marinella."

"You don't want to spend your time here at my house?"

"No."

He felt slightly offended. What had his house done to her to make her not want to stay there?

"Why, have you ever not felt right at my place?

"That's just it."

"I don't understand."

"I've always felt so good at your place. Maybe too good."

"So what?"

"I feel as if the place would affect my decisions; it would end up influencing me."

"What about me? Doesn't it influence me?"

"Less so, relatively speaking, because it's your home."

"I get it. You want the game to be played on a neutral field."

In Livia's silence he could sense the effort she was making not to answer him the way he deserved.

"I'm sorry, that was stupid, what I just said," he continued. "Let's do this. When we meet at the airport, we'll decide together where we should go, then we'll go straight there, without coming back here first. Okay?"

"Okay."

"See you tomorrow."

"See you tomorrow."

He hung up but remained next to the telephone, thinking about what Livia had said.

So the house would influence her! What kind of bullshit was that? Four walls don't influence anything! They're just walls like any others, nothing more. Good and bad houses that determine the happiness or misfortune of the people living in them exist only in American movies. And, come to think of it, even furniture had no effect. That is, as long as one didn't want it to.

In other words, unless one wanted expressly to be influenced by it. And in that case, anything at all, like, for example, the statue Livia had bought for him in Fiacca . . .

He picked it up.

About five inches tall, it represented a little boy with a cheerful, urchinlike face, carrying a basket of fish on his shoulder. It was no work of art, but it had a certain grace. Indeed Livia had bought it for the expression of the face: wise, open, intelligent. Then he suddenly remembered what she'd whispered to him as she was handing it to him:

"If we have a son one day, I would like one like this."

How many years had passed since then? Ten? Fifteen? Feeling suddenly overwhelmed with emotion, he realized that Livia was right.

It wasn't the house in itself, but all the memories, the griefs and joys, the hopes and disappointments, the tears and laughter, that influenced them, and how!

When he went to put the little statue back, it slipped out of his hand and fell to the floor. He bent down to pick it up, cursing the saints.

The head alone had come off, a clean break at the neck. There was no other damage. He tried putting it back on: a perfect fit. Not even the tiniest chip had been lost.

So he started looking for the all-purpose glue, found it, sat down and, paying very careful attention, stuck the head back onto the body. He felt pleased with himself. The reattachment came out perfectly, even though he was not very good with his hands. He set the statuette down on the table and got up to go pack his suitcase.

He would be away for at least four days with Livia. But the moment he took the bag down from atop the armoire, he fell into the doldrums and no longer felt like packing.

He would have all the time in the world to do it the following morning.

He decided to stay out on the veranda until sleep came
over him.

The next morning he woke up later than usual, after eight.
Apparently his brain and body already felt like they were on
vacation. He took a long shower and, after shaving, grabbed
his razor, soap, comb, and other things he needed for personal maintenance, put them in an elegant black toilet kit that
Livia had given him, and put it all into the suitcase. Then he
opened the armoire and started picking out some shirts. By
nine o'clock the suitcase was ready. He shut it, carried it out
to the car, and put it in the trunk.

Should he stop by the police station? Or just get into the
car without telling anyone and, if anything, phone in to headquarters from outside?

Perhaps it was best to call and let them know he was leaving. As he was lifting the receiver, he saw the little statue. He
picked it up and examined it.

The head fit perfectly, but all around the neck was a very
fine line, thin as a hair, unmistakably revealing the break and
subsequent repair.

Of course, seen from a distance, the statuette looked whole,
perfect. But from up close . . .

Too bad, he thought, putting it back where it had been.
The important thing was that he had saved it and didn't have
to throw it away.

He picked up the receiver and heard someone speaking. Had
the lines crossed? He immediately recognized Catarella's voice.

"Hullo? Hullo? Whoozat onna line?"

"Montalbano here, Cat."

"But djou call me, sir?"

"No, Cat, I was about to call you, but you were already on the line."

"So howsit I answered witout you callin' me?"

"You didn't answer; apparently you were calling me when . . . Listen, never mind, forget about it. I was calling to tell you I'm not coming in to the office because I'm about to leave for—"

"You can't leave, Chief, assolutely not!"

"Why not?"

"'Cause summon's been killed."

It was like a punch in the face.

"Where?"

" 'Zackly where the Montelusa road comes inna town."

The inspector had been hoping that it had happened outside their police jurisdiction. Whereas now they would have to deal with it.

"Do you know what his name was?"

"Fazio tol' me, but I can't remember now . . . Wait. . . . Whass a blue stone called?"

A fine time for a quiz!

"I dunno, Cat. A sapphire?"

"Nossir."

"Amethyst?"

"Nossir, sounds like fusilli."

"Lazuli? Lap—"

" 'Ass it, Chief! Mr. Lazuli was killed."

"Listen, isn't Inspector Augello there?"

"No, Chief, Isspector Augello's not onna premisses in so much as they took 'im to the hospital lass night."

"Oh my God! What happened to him?"

"To him poissonally in poisson, nuttin, Chief. But they hadda take the little kid. They took him to the podiatric hospital."

The inspector weighed his options. If he left the house at once, he would have about half an hour to help out Fazio before he had to leave for the Punta Raisi Airport. Yes, half an hour should be enough. He didn't know of anyone named Lazuli or Lazulli, nor had he ever heard of any such name. Wait, hadn't there been some recent mention of a Fasulo? Maybe it was a settling of accounts between drug dealers. He could certainly leave the matter in Fazio's hands. In any case, Augello would have to return from the hospital sooner or later, and he could take over from there.

"Tell me where Fazio is."

Catarella told him.

When he got there he had to fight his way through a throng of photographers, journalists, and television cameramen blocking the view of a Fiat Panda that had crashed into a tree at the side of the road. Gallo was directing the traffic of cars coming and going to and from Montelusa. Galluzzo was trying to keep away the curious onlookers who were pulling up and getting out of their cars to see what had happened. Fazio was talking to Galluzzo's brother-in-law, who was a journalist for TeleVigàta. Montalbano managed to go up to the Panda and noticed that it was empty. He took a better look. Blood was spattered on the dashboard and the headrest of the driver's seat.

Fazio, who had seen him arrive, came up to him.

"Where's the corpse?"

"The victim's not dead, Chief. But I don't think he'll make

it. They took him to Montelusa Hospital, but I don't know if he got there alive."

"Was it you who called the ambulance?"

"Me? Are you kidding? By the time we got here it was all over. When they shot him there was traffic all around, a big mess. Two or three cars pulled over, one of 'em called 118, another called us . . ."

"Did anyone see anything?"

"Yessir. There's one eyewitness. I had him tell me what he saw, took down his name and address, and let him go."

"What did he tell you?"

"Said he saw a high-powered motorcycle come up along-side the Panda, and then the car swerved and the biker sped away."

"Did he get a look at his face?"

"The screen on the helmet covered his whole face."

"How about the license plate, for what it's worth?"

"He didn't take it down."

"Listen, Fazio, I need to tell you something. When Catarella called me, I was about to leave for three or four days. Since I think you and Augello can manage things quite well—"

Fazio looked stunned.

"But, Chief—"

"Listen, Fazio, I really need to go away for three days. In any case, I think this Lazuli—"

"Lazuli?"

"What, isn't that his name?"

"No, Chief, it's somebody you wanted to meet. His name is Lapis, Tommaso Lapis. The guy from the Benevolence Association. Remember?"

At that exact moment everyone arrived: the Forensics team, the prosecutor, and Dr. Pasquano, who started cursing

like a madman as soon as he realized he'd been summoned
needlessly.

Montalbano realized he was lost. It was already ten-thirty.
If he left at once, racing at a speed he was utterly incapable of,
he might just make it to Punta Raisi by noon. The best thing
was to forewarn Livia that he would be late. He asked Fazio
for his cell phone and dialed.

"The telephone of the person you are trying to reach . . ."

Right. At that hour Livia was at the airport and about to
board the plane. Or maybe already in the air.

What to do? Send one of the station's cars, paying for the
gas out of his own pocket? That would certainly send Livia
into a rage. They had decided on something quite different.
From Punta Raisi they were supposed to head off to a place
they would choose on the spot. No, that would immediately
jeopardize things.

At this point there was no choice but to wait until noon,
at which time Livia would turn her cell phone back on, and
they could agree on a plan.

"Fazio, it seems to me we're just wasting time here."

"I think so, too."

"Phone the hospital and find out what condition Lapis
is in."

"Chief, they won't tell me because of this privacy stuff."

"Let's go there in my car."

At the hospital they were able to talk to a doctor friend.

"We don't think he's going to make it," said the doctor.

"How many times was he shot?"

"Just once, but it was devastating. It must have been a
large-caliber weapon. The shot was fired through the open car
window. It entered the left jawbone, blew off half his face, and
exited just above the right eye."

Montalbano then asked a question that made the doctor balk.

"Did it also blow off his upper teeth?"

"Yes. Why?"

"Just curious. So you think he's not—"

"It's a matter of hours at this point."

"So where to now?"

"To Vigàta. To the station."

They got back in the car and drove off.

"Why'd you ask him about the teeth?" said Fazio. "Do you think there could be a connection with the killing of the girl with the tattoo?"

"Since you're so good at asking questions, why don't you try to be as good at answering them?"

"Hey, hey, Chief, why so touchy? I can understand how you'd be upset 'cause this has all put a hitch in your plans, but these things happen, you know, what can you do about it? It's in our jurisdiction!"

"Go back, immediately!"

"To the hospital?"

"No, to the commissioner's office."

Maybe the solution to the problem lay in the word Fazio had used: "jurisdiction."

Pulling into the parking lot of Montelusa Central, he told Fazio to wait for him in the car and then dashed up to the anteroom of Commissioner Bonetti-Alderighi. Where, inevitably, he ran into Dr. Lattes, who, upon seeing him, came forward with open arms. What? Now that he was no longer investigating Benevolence, was he no longer the reprobate and excommunicate?

"Dear Inspector!"

"The family's all fine, thanks to the Blessed Virgin. Listen, I would like to speak with the commissioner. It's extremely urgent."

Dr. Lattes made a disconsolate face.

"But he's in Rome! Didn't you know?"

"No. When will he be back?"

"Day after tomorrow."

"Good-bye."

"Give my best to your loved ones!"

The inspector went out cursing. His intention was to present the attempted murder of Lapis and the killing of the tattooed girl as closely connected. As a result, he, Montalbano, would be forced to reopen the investigation of Benevolence. What did Mr. C'mishner think about this? Surely Bonetti-Alderighi, terrified at the thought of Montalbano resuming his shuffling with elephantine grace between monsignors and devout souls, would have passed the case on, as a matter of "jurisdiction," to Di Nardo or someone under him. And he, Montalbano, would have been free to go wherever he pleased.

But things, unfortunately, had not turned out that way.

"So where to now?"

"To the station."

Seeing the inspector even gloomier than before, Fazio didn't dare open his mouth. They'd gone a couple of miles in silence when the inspector said:

"Let's go back."

"Back?" asked Fazio, between dismay and anger.

"Back, back. After all, it's my car and I'm paying for the gas!"

"Are we going back to the commissioner's?"

"No, we're going to the Free Channel's studios."

He burst in so furiously that the girl at the reception desk took fright.

"Oh my God, Inspector Montalbano, you really—"

"Is Zito in?"

"He's in his office. He's alone."

He pushed the door open with such force that it slammed against the wall, and the newsman leapt from his chair.

"What is this? Has the Catarella method been adopted by your entire police force?"

"Sorry, Nicolò, I'm in a really big hurry. Have you heard about the attempted murder of a man named Lapis?"

"Yes, I just broadcast the news half an hour ago."

"Do you know who he was?"

"Was?"

"Yes, I was just at the hospital. He's got only a few hours to live. So, who was he?"

"A decent fellow. Forty years old, unmarried. Up until last year he had a fabrics store. Then business turned bad and he had to close it. There's no explanation for the shooting. Maybe a terrible case of mistaken identity."

"No explanation?"

Zito's eyes sparkled and he tensed in his chair.

"Why, have *you* got an explanation for it?"

"I may."

"What is it?"

"Do you know of an organization called Benevolence, founded by Monsignor Pisicchio?"

"No . . . or maybe yes . . . I've vaguely heard it mentioned. They're involved in rescuing young women who—"

"Exactly. Did you know that Tommaso Lapis was the guy whose job it was to convince these girls to abandon the life they were leading and put their trust in Monsignor Pisicchio's organization?"

"No, I didn't know. So you think some pimp—"

"Wait. Did you know that the girl with the moth tattoo, the one killed by Morabito, had almost certainly been taken in by Benevolence?"

"Holy shit!"

"Exactly. So you, Nicolò, have got to start making a lot of noise about this connection, immediately. Trumpets blaring. Because, you see, everyone at Benevolence is on the take. Half a day is all someone like you would need to figure things out. But you gotta start raising the roof right now."

"Why?"

"As I said, I'm in a really big hurry, Nicolò. In fact, what time is it?"

"Ten past twelve."

Matre santa, he was late!

"Can I make a phone call?"

"Sure."

"The telephone of the person you are trying to reach may be . . ."

18

They found Mimì Augello waiting for them in the main doorway of the station. He had the face of someone who hadn't slept a wink all night.

"How's the baby?"

"Better now."

"What was wrong with him?"

"Some chickenshit that Beba blew all out of proportion."

"Let's go into my office," said the inspector.

"Oh," said Augello, "I wanted to tell you that the hospital just called. Lapis is dead."

"So," began Montalbano, as soon as they had all sat down. "We have to pick up the Benevolence investigation where we left off. I had asked you both to dig up as much information as possible on—"

"Guglielmo Piro, Michela Zicari, Anna Degregorio, Gerlando Cugno, and Stefania Rizzo," Fazio recited from memory. "Tommaso Lapis was also on the list, but we have to cross him off due to circumstances beyond our control."

"Now, however, we've got no more time to waste on information. We have to move into action. I want to see all of them, one by one, here at the station, starting now. The first on the list should be our beloved Cavaliere Guglielmo Piro."

"One minute," said Mimì. "Shouldn't we inform the prosecutor?"

"We should, but we won't."

"Why not?"

"Because it's ninety-nine percent certain that Tommaseo will find a rash of quibbles to waste our time with."

"So let him waste it. The important thing is for him not to block us."

"Mimì, first of all, I'm in a really big hurry. Secondly, my fear is precisely that Tommaseo will be forced by some superior of his to block us."

"Why are you in such a hurry?"

"None of your fucking business."

Mimì stood up, bowed to Montalbano, then sat back down.

"Faced with so exhaustive an explanation of your reasons," he said, "I declare myself fully satisfied. So you think there's a connection between the killings of Lapis and the girl with the tattoo?"

"It seems clear to me."

"Where's all this clarity come from?"

"From the fact that the shot that killed Lapis followed the exact same trajectory as the shot that killed the girl."

"Could be a coincidence."

"No, Mimì, it's a message. Clear to any who want to read it. For those who don't, it's only a coincidence, as you say."

"And what does the message say?"

"I killed this man the same way he got that girl killed."

"But maybe—"

"Mimì, you're making me lose too much time. Come on, Fazio, get moving. In fact, you give 'im a hand, too, Mimì."

It was already two o'clock. He tried calling Livia again. Nothing. Only the usual recorded female voice. The phone rang. Want to bet it's her? He was ready to beg her forgiveness, even get down on his knees in the presence of the whole police force.

"Ahh Chief! That'd be summon who says 'is name is Antonio Dona and 'd like to talk t'you poissonally in poisson."

He'd never met anyone one named Antonio Dona in his life. But he took the call.

"Hello, this is Don Antonio, do you remember me?"

Of course he remembered him! The boxing priest!

"What can I do for you?"

"I'm on my way to your office with Katya."

"Where are you right now?"

"About three-quarters of the way there."

But, if Katya came to the station, she might run into someone from Benevolence.

"Listen, Father, do you know where Marinella is?"

"Of course."

"Perhaps it's better if we meet there. There's a bar, and at this hour there won't be anyone there. You'll see it right away; it's got a great big sign."

Catarella saw him shoot past like a rocket.

Katya Lissenko was a very fine-looking girl. The forms of her solid, artfully shaped body were practically bursting out of her clothes, even though they were hidden and humbled inside a pair of baggy jeans and a big floppy sweater. It was clear how poor Signor Graceffa could have lost his head over her.

"Katya decided to come talk to you as soon as we heard that Tommaso Lapis had been shot. And on the way here we learned that he died," Don Antonio began.

"A preliminary question," said Montalbano. "Do you, Katya, want this meeting to remain private, or are you willing to testify in court?"

Katya exchanged glances with Don Antonio.

"I'm willing to testify."

"But until you do," Don Antonio cut in, "I think it's best if you stay with us. Katya has managed to meet a fine young man who is putting her up. They're very fond of each other. But I'm afraid of what could happen, Inspector."

"You're absolutely right. So, Katya, shall I begin with my questions?"

"All right."

"Why the moth tattoo?"

"In Schelkovo, the agency I turned to for help in expatriating used to do that. Since we would leave in small groups, usually four girls at a time, five at the most, they made each group take a different tattoo."

"A kind of branding."

Katya's beautiful face darkened.

"Right. Like they do with animals. Anyway, that's what we were for them—work animals. And we needed the work to help out our families, who had sold everything they had. We went through some terrible times in Russia. They made us study a bit of dance and immediately we were off to Italy to work the nightclubs. There were four girls in our group, same as the number of wings on the moth that was tattooed on our shoulder blades."

"How much did you earn, on average, in the nightclubs?"

"The money we earned went directly to pay off our debt to

the agency in Schelkovo, which also took care of finding us an apartment together in Italy. To earn enough to be able to send some back home, we had to go with clients after closing time."

She blushed.

"I see. Where did you meet Tommaso Lapis?"

"At a nightclub in Palermo. First we were sent to Viareggio, Grosseto, and then Salerno. Lapis talked mostly to Sonya. Several times. Finally, one day, when we were all at home, Sonya told us that Mr. Lapis had offered to have us all move to Montelusa, where a charitable organization would take care of us and have us work as home care assistants, housekeepers, cleaning women. Honest jobs that might lead to something."

"And who was going to settle the debt with the agency?"

"Lapis said not to worry about it. He would have his friends take care of it."

Mafiosi, apparently.

"The fact remains," Katya continued, "that our families in Russia didn't suffer any reprisals. Because this was what the people at the agency were always threatening us with. If one of you escapes, they would say, her family's gonna pay."

"In short, you accepted Lapis's offer."

"Yes. But Lapis wanted us to show up at the Benevolence office saying that we had come there on our own and not mention that he had suggested it to us. And he ordered us not to come all at the same time."

It was clear: Lapis wanted to hide his role as principal inspiration and organizer of the group.

"Why, when you arrived, were you and Irina so terrified?"

"Who, us?" said Katya, completely confused.

Apparently this was a little extra color added by Cavaliere Piro.

"So, Sonya arrived after the two of you?"

"Yes."

"By any chance, was your fourth companion Zin?"

"Zinaida Gregorenko, yes."

"How come she never came and joined you at Benevolence?"

Katya gave him a puzzled look.

"What do you mean, she never came? She was the fourth
to arrive!"

Cavaliere Piro had neglected to tell him this. So the cavaliere, too, was neck-deep in it.

"Then what happened?"

"What happened was that the day after the four of us were
brought together, Mr. Lapis took us aside and told us what he
had in mind. He was going to place us in different homes, and
we were supposed to keep our eyes open and see if there was any
jewelry or money. And then, when the time was right, to steal it
and disappear. Afterwards, he would take care of relocating us in
another town and selling the stuff. The person who carried out
the robbery was entitled to twenty-five percent of the proceeds."

"Did all of you accept?"

"Sonya did right away. But I think she was already in
agreement with him before leaving the nightclub. Then Irina
and Zin also accepted. Then I did, too."

"Why?"

"Where would I go without the other girls? It was important for us to stay together. But I secretly promised myself that
I would run away the first chance I got. Which I did. I never
stole anything. Then Zin also quit, but for other reasons."

"What sort of reasons?"

"She fell in love and went to live with her boyfriend."

"And how did Lapis take this?"

"Badly. But he couldn't do anything about it. Because the man Zin was with was a dangerous criminal and threatened to tell the police the whole story."

"When you heard on television that a girl was found dead in an illegal dump, did you realize immediately that they were talking about Sonya?"

Katya looked at him saucer-eyed.

"Sonya?!"

"It wasn't her?"

"No, it was Zin who was killed!"

Now it was Montalbano's turn to look saucer-eyed.

"But wasn't Zin out of the loop by then?"

"She was. But she needed money to pay for her boyfriend's lawyer after he ended up in jail. And Lapis took advantage of this to persuade her to come back to him. He got her hired by a housecleaning business. One of Zin's jobs was to clean the apartment of that shop owner. Eventually she realized he had a lot of money in the house, especially on Saturday nights. But Zin imposed one condition: that, after this job, Lapis was not to show his face anymore. But then . . ."

Two big tears rolled down her cheeks. Don Antonio put his hand on her shoulder for a moment.

"But how did you find out all these things?"

"Every now and then I call Sonya."

"Excuse me, but Sonya could find out where the calls are coming from, couldn't she?"

"I only use public phones when I talk to her."

For the moment he had no more questions for her. What he'd learned was more than enough.

"Listen, miss, I am extremely grateful to you for what you've told me. If I needed to talk to you again, how—"

"Just call me," said Don Antonio. "But I have one request, if I may."

"Go ahead."

"I want you to send all those crooks from Benevolence to jail. Their presence is a blot on the clean, hard work of thousands of honest volunteers."

"I will certainly try to do that," said the inspector, standing up.

Katya and Don Antonio also stood up.

"I wish you a serene and happy life," Montalbano said to Katya. And he embraced her.

Before leaving the bar he tried calling Livia from the establishment's phone. Nothing.

Catarella again saw him flash by like a rocket.

"Ahh Chie—"

"I'm not here, I'm not here!"

He didn't even sit down at his desk. Still standing up, he tried calling Livia again. The usual recording. He became convinced that Livia, after waiting for him in vain, had gone back home to Boccadasse, feeling disconsolate, maybe even desperate. What kind of night was she going to have, all alone in Boccadasse? What kind of shit of a man was Salvo Montalbano, who would leave her in the lurch like that?

He searched through a drawer for a small piece of paper, found it, grabbed the outside line, and dialed a number.

"Punta Raisi Airport Police? Is Inspector Capuano there? Could you put him on? This is Inspector Montalbano."

"Salvo, what is it?"

"Listen, Capuà, you absolutely have to get me a seat on

this evening's flight to Genoa. You also have to make the ticket for me."

"Wait."

Multiplication tables for six. Six curses. Multiplication tables for seven. Seven curses. Multiplication tables for eight. Eight curses.

"Montalbano? There's room. I'll have somebody book the flight for you."

"To say you're an angel is not saying enough, Capuà."

No sooner had he set down the receiver than Fazio and Augello came in, out of breath.

"Catarella told us you were back, and so—" Mimì began.

"What time is it?" Montalbano interrupted him.

"Almost four."

He had one hour, more or less, at his disposal.

"We've summoned them all," said Fazio. "Guglielmo will be here at five on the dot, and the others will arrive after that."

"Now listen to me very carefully, because as soon as I've finished talking, the investigation will be in your hands. Yours, Mimì, and Fazio's."

"And what are you going to do?"

"I'm going to disappear, Mimì. And don't get any ideas about tracking me down and breaking my balls, because, even if you succeed in finding me, I won't talk to either of you. Is that clear?"

"Perfectly."

Montalbano then recounted what Katya had told him.

"Evidently," he concluded, "Cavaliere Piro was in league with Lapis. I don't know about the others. It's up to you to find out. It's also obvious that Lapis was murdered out of revenge. He had forced Zin to go back to thieving, and the girl ended up getting shot by Morabito. So Zin's boyfriend, who apparently was madly in love with her, killed Lapis in turn."

"It won't be easy to put a name on this killer," said Augello.

"I'll tell you his name, Mimì. It's Peppi Cannizzaro. A repeat offender."

Fazio and Augello looked at him dumbfounded.

"All right, but . . . he won't be easy to find," said Augello.

"I'll even give you his address: Via Palermo 16, in Gallotta. You want me also to tell you what size shoe he wears?"

"Oh no you don't!" Mimì burst out. "You have to tell us how you managed to—"

"None of your fucking business."

Mimì stood up, made a bow, and sat back down.

"Your explanations, Professor, never leave any room for doubt."

The telephone rang.

"Ahh Chief Chief! Ahh Chief Chief!"

Must be something serious.

"What's happened, Cat?"

"Hizzoner the c'mishner called! From Rome, he called!"

"Why didn't you put his call through to me?"

" 'Cause he tol' me to only tell you how and whereats he assolutely wants you to be assolutely onna premisses at five-fifteen onna dot 'cause he's gonna call back from Rome."

"When he rings, put him straight through."

He looked at Fazio and Augello.

"It was the commissioner, calling from Rome. He's going to call back at five-fifteen."

"What's he want?" asked Mimì.

"He's going to advise us to handle the matter with extreme caution. It's explosive stuff. Listen, Fazio, is Gallo here?"

"He's here."

"Tell him to fill up the tank on one of the squad cars. I'll pay for it myself. And to make himself available."

Fazio stood up and walked out.

"I'm not convinced," said Mimì.

"By what?"

"The commissioner's phone call. He's going to make us pass the baton."

"Mimì, if that happens, what can you do?"

Augello heaved a deep sigh.

"There are moments when I wish I was Don Quixote."

"There's an essential difference, Mimì. Don Quixote thought that windmills were monsters, whereas what we're dealing with really are monsters, but they pretend they're windmills."

Fazio returned.

"All taken care of."

Nobody felt like talking. At five o'clock Catarella announced that Signor Giro had arrived.

"That must be Piro," said Fazio. "What should I do?"

"Show him into Mimì's room. And make him wait, the pig."

At a quarter past five, the telephone rang.

"Ahh Chief Chief!"

"Put him on," said Montalbano, turning on the speakerphone.

"Good afternoon, Mr. Commi—"

"Montalbano? Listen to me very carefully, and don't say a word. I'm in Rome, in the undersecretary's office, and I haven't got any time to waste. I've been informed of what's happening down there. Among other things, you didn't even bother to notify Prosecutor Tommaseo of your impulsive summons of the directors of Benevolence. As of this moment, the case is turned over to the chief of the flying squad, Inspector Filiberto. Is that clear? You are not to concern yourself any longer with this case. In no way, shape, or form. Understood? Good-bye."

"QED," commented Augello.

The other telephone rang.

"Who could that be?" the inspector wondered.

"The Pope, to tell you you've been excommunicated," said Mimì.

Montalbano picked up the receiver.

"Yes?" he said, keeping to generalities.

"Montalbano? I don't think we've had a chance to meet yet. I'm Emanuele Filiberto, the new chief of the flying squad. I'm wondering how far you got with your investigation."

"As far as you like."

"Namely?"

"For example, would you like me to tell you the name and surname of the girl who was killed?"

"Why not?"

"Would you like me to tell you that Tommaso Lapis was the leader of a band of female thieves?"

"Why not?"

"Would you like me to tell you the name of Lapis's killer?"

"Why not?"

"Would you like me to tell you what connections there were between Lapis and a benevolent association called, indeed, Benevolence, which has protectors in very, very high places? Or should I stop and not tell you anything more?"

"Why stop at the best part?"

"A few minutes ago the commissioner phoned me from Rome."

"He phoned me, too."

"What did he say to you?"

"He said to proceed carefully."

"And that's all?"

"And that's all. I'm particularly interested in the connection with the benevolent association. Have you seen the Free Channel today?"

"No. What did they do?"

"They're making a really big deal out of all this. Out of the scams of this Piro guy. Just think, in the space of three hours they broadcast two special editions."

"All right, then, my second-in-command, Inspector Augello, is going to come to your office straightaway. He knows everything."

"I'll be waiting for him."

Montalbano set down the telephone and looked at Fazio and Mimì, who had heard everything.

"Maybe there is still a judge in Berlin," he said, standing up. "Mimì, bring Cavaliere Piro along with you. He'll be our token of friendship to Filiberto. So long, boys. See you in a few days."

Gallo was waiting for him in the corridor.

"Can you make it to Punta Raisi in an hour?"

"Yessir, I can, if I turn on the siren."

It was worse than at Indianapolis. Gallo had fifty-eight firsts and fourteen seconds.

"Don't you have any baggage?" asked Capuano.

Montalbano slapped himself hard on the forehead. He'd forgotten his suitcase in the trunk of his own car.

———

Once he was in the air, a wicked hunger came over him.

"Is there anything to eat?" he begged the stewardess.

She brought him a box of cookies. He made do with them.

Then he began to review the words he would have to say to make Livia forgive him. The third time he repeated them, they sounded so convincing to him, so moving, that he very nearly broke out in tears.

———

He put his ear against the door to Livia's apartment, heart beating so wildly that it risked waking up everyone in the building. *Boom-boom, boom-boom, boom-boom.* His face was all twisted up, perhaps from the emotion, perhaps because of the box of cookies. He couldn't hear anything on the other side of the door. No television, no sound at all. Absolute silence.

Maybe she'd already gone to bed, tired and angry for having traveled all that way for nothing. So he rang the door-bell with a slightly trembling finger. Nothing. He rang again. Nothing.

In the very first year of their relationship, he and Livia had exchanged keys to their respective homes, which they always carried with them.

He took his key, opened the door, and went inside.

He realized at once that Livia wasn't there. That she had not been back to her apartment since leaving that morning. The first thing he saw was her cell phone on the console in the vestibule. She'd forgotten it, and that was why she hadn't picked up for any of his calls.

What now? Where had she gone? How was he going to find her? He felt dejected, overwhelmed all at once by fatigue, which made him weak in the knees. He went into the bedroom and lay down. Closed his eyes. He suddenly reopened them, as the telephone on the nightstand was ringing.

"Hello?"

"I knew it! I knew it! I sensed that you would be so stupid, so imbecilic as to go off to Boccadasse!"

It was Livia, and she was in a rage.

"Livia! You have no idea how hard I've been looking for you! You nearly drove me insane! Where are you calling from? Where are you?"

"When I realized you weren't coming, I took the bus. Where do you think I am? At your place! Don't you see that every time you insist on doing things your way you end up making such a stinking mess that—"

"Listen, Livia, if you hadn't forgotten your cell phone here, I would have . . ."

And so began a great big squabble, just like old times.

AUTHOR'S NOTE

This novel is made up. What I mean is that the characters, their names, and the situations in which they find themselves have no reference to any real-life persons. There is no doubt, however, that the novel is born of a specific reality. And thus someone may happen to think they recognize him- or herself in a character or situation, though I assure any and all that should this happen, it is merely by an unfortunately and utterly unintended coincidence.

I wish to thank Maurizio Assalto, for having sent me a newspaper article, and his girlfriend, Larissa, for some of the stories she told me.

A. C.

NOTES

4 "Garruso" . . . "Garrufo": *Garruso* is a common insult in Sicilian that means "rogue, rascal." Literally, it means "homosexual."

4 the government was thinking about building a bridge over the Strait of Messina: This has long been a pet project of Silvio Berlusconi, past and present prime minister of Italy and a business tycoon in his own right. The bridge project is one of several grandiose public works by which Berlusconi would like to monumentalize his dubious stewardship of the Italian nation.

9 *Matre santa*: "Holy mother" in Sicilian dialect.

30 immediately started firing blindly, feeling perhaps empowered to do so by the recent law on self-defense: On January 24, 2006, in a highly controversial move, the right-wing Berlusconi government passed a reform of article 52 of the Constitution, easing the restrictions on justifiable self-defense. The reform followed the relaxation of the requirements for the right to bear arms and has led to a number of apparently needless and avoidable deaths.

79 "The *ragioniere* Curcuraci": *Ragioniere* is a largely meaningless title given to accountants whose specialization does not go beyond that provided by vocational school. A fully certified accountant is called a *contabile*.

97 *Nuttata persa e figlia femmina*: Literally, "a wasted night and it's a girl," the expression means "a lot of time wasted and nothing to show for it."

98 little street called Via Platone. Given that he was in a philosophical neighborhood: Platone is Italian for Plato, and Empedocle is, of course, the pre-Socratic philosopher Empedocles, who was a Sicilian from Agrigentum, the ancient name of Agrigento, Camilleri's model for the town of Montelusa. The model for Vigàta is Porto Empedocle, Camilleri's hometown.

104 "to combine benefit and delight": Montalbano is alluding to the famous dictum articulated by Horace (65–8 BC) in his *Ars Poetica*: *"Aut prodesse volunt aut delectare poetae / aut simul et iucunda et idonea dicere vitae,"* (ll. 333–34), according to which poetry should both benefit and delight the reader.

109 "cululùchira" . . . A buttock tattoo?: *Culu* in Sicilian (*culo* in Italian) means "buttocks."

132 "I just thought of another cavaliere who uses his younger brother as a front man for himself. It's become a widespread practice.": Montalbano is referring to the fact that Prime Minister Silvio Berlusconi, commonly known as *il cavaliere*, has very often used his younger brother Paolo to represent his interests in order to avoid the appearance of conflicts of interest. Among other things, Paolo Berlusconi has run newspapers for his brother (*Il Giornale* and *La Notte*) and sat on the board of a number of major concerns (Mediolanum Assicurazioni and Standa).

132 "Even a homicide, with these new laws, can prove 'unactionable.' ": See note for page 30.

154 But why, in 2006, would a mayor still want to name a street after Atilius Regulus?: Marcus Atilius Regulus was a general and consul in the First Punic War (256 BC).

166 "I did. I noticed a strong burning smell, and —"/"I smell it, too": The original text has a double entendre here: In Sicilian, to "smell something burning" (*sentire feto di bruciato*) means "to smell a rat."

167 the quotation of Mussolini: On October 2, 1935, from the famous balcony in Palazzo Venezia in Rome, from which he normally addressed the throngs, Mussolini virtually declared war on Ethiopia in saying: "We've waited forty years, and that's enough!" He was referring, in substance, to the fact that Italy had had to repress her imperial ambitions and destiny for forty years, beginning with the first stirrings of foreign conquest in North Africa in the 1890s.

206 "one of 'em called 118": The emergency telephone number, the Italian equivalent of 911.

224 "Maybe there is still a judge in Berlin": A reference to the famous anecdote, immortalized in a poem by Andrieux, in which Frederick II of Prussia, wishing to extend the domains of the Sans-Souci, his country château, asked a miller whose property abutted the royal domain to sell it to him. When the miller refused, the king said he would seize the land outright. To which the miller defiantly replied, "Yes, if there are no judges in Berlin!"

Notes by Stephen Sartarelli